Like Night and Day

Amy walked over to the window, wondering if any of the wedding guests had arrived. She was just in time to see a beat-up silver Chevrolet pull into the wide circular driveway. It clanked and clattered. Then the driver got out, and Amy couldn't keep from gasping. He was simply gorgeous.

The boy stood for a moment, tucking the tails of his yellow oxford shirt into his jeans. His shirt-sleeves were rolled up to the elbow, revealing tanned, muscular arms. Amy smiled. This boy was as different from Colin as night from day.

Books from Scholastic
in the **Couples** series:

COUPLES

SOMETHING NEW

by M.E. Cooper

SCHOLASTIC INC.
New York Toronto London Auckland Sydney

ISBN 0-590-40794-5

12 11 10 9 8 7 6 5 4 3 2 1   7 8 9/8 0 1 2/9

Printed in the U.S.A.   01

First Scholastic printing, August 1987

SOMETHING NEW

Chapter 1

Amy Atkinson jabbed as hard as she could at the soil around her tomato plants.

"Hey!"

She paused at the sound of her sister's voice and lazily swept beads of perspiration off her forehead with the back of her hand. Turning toward the house, she could see her sixteen-year-old sister, Susan, peering at her from the old wicker armchair on the back porch. "There are faster routes to China, you know," Susan kidded her.

Amy flashed her sister an exasperated look, then turned her attention back to the garden. She bent down and carefully extracted three earthworms from the soft ground, then transferred them to a safe zone two feet away before resuming her digging.

She sighed, dug deeper, closed her eyes and thought back to another hot summer a couple of years earlier, before her parents divorced, before she had fallen madly in love with Colin Edwards. She'd been so together then, the steady one in the family, the one her skittish little sister came to for comfort and advice. Lately it seemed like they had changed places.

"I mean it, Ame," Susan persisted, stretching her long, slender legs out in front of her and wiggling her toes. "What are you getting so worked up about? It's only Dad who's late calling — not Colin. You know Dad, he's probably holed up in the library." Susan fanned her face with her hand and tipped her chair back at a dangerous angle to regard her sister closely. "So what's the big deal?"

Amy sighed again. She lifted her arm and shoved back a long strand of blonde hair that had drifted down onto her forehead and settled annoyingly on her nose.

There was *no* big deal. But she couldn't get rid of the gloomy thoughts that had been drifting in and out of her head all afternoon. If she couldn't depend on her father, what made her think she could depend on Colin? She knew she was being unreasonable. Crazy, even. But her father *did* fall out of love with her mother, didn't he? So what was to keep her from thinking that Colin would never fall out of love with her?

Her eyes clouded. Almost a year had passed since her parents' divorce, yet it still hurt.

Amy looked over at Sam, the Atkinsons' dachshund. He had curled himself into a circle at her feet and was sleeping peacefully. "At least one of us is calm, Sammy," she whispered, bending

2

down to shoo away a stubborn August fly from his shoulder. She eased herself down next to him on the grass and ran her hand over his soft, smooth fur.

She remembered the day her parents had brought Sam home. She and Susan had been disappointed — they had both wanted a cute, cuddly puppy, one that would grow into a big dog. But of course they had both instantly fallen in love with the little waddling dachshund. Oddly enough, she'd been feeling like a little girl again lately. She played weird games with herself, telling herself that something good — or bad — would happen if something else came through for her. If it rains before four, he loves me, if this flower dies tomorrow, it means he doesn't love me anymore.

That's why she wanted the phone to ring when it was supposed to, at three o'clock sharp. She wanted to talk to her father, but it was more than that. The call was supposed to *do* something for her. In her game, it was the guarantee Colin would love her forever.

Amy stretched her legs out and bent at the waist to hold onto her ankles, then tucked her legs into a more comfortable position. She felt a trickle of perspiration making its way down her back, and she pressed her worn turquoise polo shirt against her skin to blot the dampness. Softly, she hummed to the Beatles song that was playing on Susan's radio.

"Let it be," Susan wailed suddenly and passionately.

Amy giggled. She and Colin were seniors, but

Susan was certainly more of an expert on love than they were — and she was only a junior. Amy's head had spun over the last year as she tried to keep track of her younger sister's crushes. Only Rich, Colin's younger brother, had dazzled Susan enough to keep her on track.

Colin. When Amy closed her eyes, she could almost taste his kisses. He'd made falling in love feel so natural. Not that he was any expert . . . this was his first time, too.

"Ame. A-my!" Amy's eyes popped open. Susan was squatting right in front of her. She wore a lopsided smile. "Geez," she marveled. Her purple-framed sunglasses sat perched on top of her head. Her blue eyes twinkled. Susan stood up and placed her hands smartly on her hips. "If I knew for sure that dirt and sweat would make *me* look that dreamy-eyed, *I'd* take up gardening, too."

Amy grinned.

"Do you actually believe — " Susan said, swallowing a giggle, "that seven days is enough time for you to get cleaned up for Andrea's wedding?" She pursed her lips, raised her eyebrows, and spoke very fast. "Or, dear sister, are you so lovesick you forgot that a week from today we're going to be bridesmaids in our favorite cousin's wedding?"

Amy tilted her head and scratched an itch just below her ear. Thinking about the wedding made her pulse race. She hadn't forgotten about it. She *couldn't* have! Aside from her immediate family and Colin, Andrea Moore was her favorite person in the whole world. Now, thinking about her cousin and the upcoming wedding, she cheered up completely, as if the thunderstorm raging inside her had moved out to sea, leaving the sun in its wake.

"Not only will I be *clean* by then," she promised, "I'll be smiling, too!"

"Well, that's a relief," Susan said. "Living with you lately has been like riding a seesaw."

Amy let out a good-natured groan as she got to her feet and began gathering her tools. She plucked a rag from the back pocket of her cut-offs and painstakingly began wiping her gardening rake and trowel. For the moment her troubles were forgotten. She felt like her old, confident self again — the girl Colin had fallen in love with.

Sometimes it felt like the more she loved Colin, the less confidence she had in herself. Amy *hated* feeling so insecure. Why couldn't she have both — love and confidence — instead of constantly swinging on a pendulum between them? Now, at least, the pendulum was in mid-swing. But how long would that last?

"Sam!" she cried suddenly, dropping her tools. "No!"

Sam had bulleted deep into the yard, closing in on a squirrel frozen with fright by the hedge. The squirrel's bushy tail twitched, and he looked at Sam through narrowed eyes.

Amy stumbled toward Sam, reaching for his collar. Susan nearly flew down the porch steps.

The squirrel disappeared under the hedge before Sam even got close. Amy drooped with relief. But a moment later, Sam was thrashing in the grass near her feet, whining, poking one of his paws with his wet, black nose. Before he could wiggle away, Amy grabbed him. He winced, yipping shrilly, and she felt herself tense.

"What's wrong with him?" Susan asked. Reluctantly, she bent to look.

Amy sat down in the grass with Sam in her arms. She gripped his soft body carefully but firmly, so he couldn't get away. "Easy, sweet puppy," she comforted. He squirmed as she probed him cautiously with her fingers until he winced again. "It's his foot," Amy said. Her eyes wandered to the trowel, lying in the grass. She looked down guiltily.

The point of the trowel was bright red with blood. Amy released a small, wavering sigh. It was her fault that Sam had cut his foot — not Sam's. He'd done what was natural for him. Sam was a dog; dogs chase after little animals.

Susan came over to help Amy up. "Hey," she said comfortingly. "Don't blame yourself."

"Are you kidding?" Amy snapped. She was immediately sorry but she couldn't keep from feeling as if it were her fault. She started toward the porch.

Susan followed her, obviously holding back tears. "What do you want me to do?" Susan asked. Her arms hung limply at her sides.

"Get a towel," Amy said, in a tone meant to be apologetic. "Okay?" Holding Sam, she lowered herself into the wicker armchair and reached for the phone on the little rattan table. "I'll call the vet. Make sure the towel's clean," she called as she screen door slammed.

6

The phone rang just as her fingers touched it.

"Colin!" she said.

"Hello, adorable Amy," he whispered, "I love you."

"I love you, too, but — "

"No buts! And wait'll you hear who we've got lined up to give the Freedom Reader Workshop!"

Amy had heard all about the Freedom Readers. It was a group that Colin, Marc Harrison, and Dick Westergard, a recent graduate, were organizing to help kids in school — and out of school — improve their reading skills. The last she'd heard, they were setting a date for a training session.

"Colin — " Amy said, trying to steady herself. "I can't talk now. I have to call the vet."

"What's wrong?" Colin's voice filled with concern.

"Sam's hurt. His foot's bleeding." Amy held the receiver to her shoulder with her chin. Blinking back tears, she wrapped Sam's paw with the towel Susan had tossed to her.

"That's rough," Colin commiserated. "I'll get right off." He hesitated. "Wait a minute — Amy?"

"What?"

Colin spoke quickly. "I know this is a bad time to be asking, but I have to know now. Will you still be able to go with me to get the stuff for the posters? If we don't advertise the workshop soon, no one will know about it."

"Sure," Amy said. "I mean, maybe," she corrected herself. Sam yipped when she applied

7

pressure to the makeshift bandage. She planted a kiss between his ears. "It depends on how things go at the vet's."

"Sam'll be fine," Colin encouraged. "With you taking care of him, how could he miss?"

Amy smiled as she hung up the phone and quickly dialed the vet.

He was relieved that Sam's cut was between his toes and not on the pad of his foot where bleeding would have been a real problem. Infecton was still a concern though.

Amy promised she'd drive Sam in as soon as she could figure out a way to get him to the clinic. Her car was in the shop, and her mom was out shopping for a dress to wear to Andrea's wedding. Maybe Colin could take her.

Carefully, Amy followed the vet's instructions. Susan had struck it rich under their mother's bathroom sink: Isopropyl alcohol, cotton pads, and gauze. Enough to hold Sam until the vet could examine him later.

Susan gave Amy an approving smile. "Maybe you'll be a *real* vet someday, doc. You're doing great."

"Thanks, Sue," Amy said sincerely. But her smile soon turned downward. She couldn't get rid of the uneasy feeling that had crept over her as soon as she spoke to Colin. And now here was Susan talking about her future. Why did everyone expect so much from her?

Chapter
2

The doorbell rang. Amy took the steps two at a time, her hair streaming behind her. She flung open the door, and her first thought was what a fool she'd been. Colin was here. His eyes shone, looking at her. As usual, she'd been crazy to have worried about his love for her.

"What's that behind your back?" she asked. Colin's hands were hidden, and she was tingling with curiosity. Taking hold of his T-shirt, she pulled him into the entranceway and shut the door.

"Where?" he teased, peering over his shoulder.

Amy tried reaching behind him. He dodged her, his bent elbows swinging.

"Let me see!" she squealed.

"See what!" Colin laughed. "My eyes? My nose? My lips?" He made smacking noises and kissed her when her face dipped close enough.

His familiar, fresh scent made her shiver with pleasure.

Colin nuzzled her, and Amy wound her arms around his neck. His mouth met hers in a gentle, lingering kiss as he slipped his arms behind her back. She hardly noticed the blunt object in his hand that pressed into her shoulder. But when it clunked to the floor, she leaned back and peeked behind him, her hands still lightly resting on Colin's arms.

"Colin!" On the floor lay the biggest dog biscuit she had ever seen tied in a huge red satin bow.

"For the invalid," Colin announced. "How is the little guy? Did the vet prescribe two aspirin and plenty of O.J.?"

"Well, I kind of hoped you'd provide the ambulance," Amy answered. "If you drive us, I promise to be your best friend forever!"

"Okay, okay — I know when I've been sufficiently bribed," Colin said with a laugh.

Amy covered his face with a flurry of brief, feathery kisses. When their lips met again, they held each other as if they'd never let go. Finally they broke apart to catch their breath. Colin pulled back slightly and ran his fingers through Amy's silky blonde hair.

"Ahem." Mrs. Atkinson came into the room holding a shopping bag and a stack of interior design magazines. "It's a good thing you two are still in high school," she said. She peered over the magazines and nodded at the shopping bag. "I'd hate to think I had to run out and buy a dress for another wedding!" Winking, she headed upstairs.

Colin chuckled, but Amy stared after her mother into the empty space she'd left behind. A year ago, her mother was still married. Now, in one week, she'd be going to her brother's daughter's wedding. That would be hard for her.

Amy shuddered. How could anyone ever know if love would last?

Out of the corner of her eye, she saw Colin staring at her. Her insides churned, but she mustered a cheerful smile. He gave her an affectionate squeeze as Sam labored unsteadily onto the pillow Susan had made for him.

"How about if we take him in before we get the stuff for the posters?" Amy said, looking questioningly at Colin.

Colin shrugged agreeably. "Sounds good," he said. "Now where were we?" he teased, and Amy hugged him.

In a moment, he drew back. He studied her face with serious eyes. "Amy?" he said. Her arms rested on his waist. "What was that all about before?" He looked at her curiously. "You seemed so far away."

Amy shrugged slowly and shook her head. She pressed close to Colin's chest, and all her sadness vanished. Beneath her cheek, Colin's cotton T-shirt smelled like a summer breeze, as if it had been hung to dry in the August sun.

Business was booming at the Rose Hill Mall, especially in Ross's Art Supply Store. Kids were swooping in to take advantage of a special preschool sale.

Hot jazz blasted from the speakers. Amy's

fingers tapped in rhythm to a bluesy piano piece she didn't recognize. Sam was safe at the vet's, and she felt much better now that she was surrounded by a bustling crowd.

"What do you think?" Colin asked. He held up a floppy piece of greenish posterboard for Amy to take a good look at. "It's on sale," he reported. His voice was muffled behind it.

Amy giggled. "No wonder," she said. Colin peeked over the top of the huge flapping square.

"Okay," he said, deadpan, "give it to me straight. You think the color looks too much like pea soup, don't you?"

Amy folded with laughter. "It's fine, if you *like* pea soup," she sputtered. "But it's just not *you*. . . . As for me — " She batted her eyes over a piece she'd pulled off the shelf. A smile crossed her face. "I prefer sky blue."

"Indeed," Colin returned, raising his eyebrows. "You would choose a color that sets off your eyes." He pulled Amy toward him in the narrow aisle.

"Hey, lovebirds!" The owner of the store was taking inventory near the easels. She cast her thick auburn hair over her shoulder and grinned before issuing a feeble threat. "You guys crush that posterboard and you've bought it!"

"She means it," a familiar voice behind them said.

Amy whirled. "Brenda!"

"It's true," Brenda Austin continued. She whispered confidentially to Colin and Amy. Her hands dramatically clutched each of their arms. "I know a kid who's doing thirty to life for knocking over a pencil sharpener here." Brenda giggled and tucked a strand of fine dark hair behind her ear.

"You look great," Amy complimented. Brenda had recently broken up with her long-time boyfriend Brad Davidson, but she seemed to be in remarkably good spirits.

Brenda looked grateful. "Thanks." She grinned at Amy.

"So what are you doing here?" Amy asked. "Stocking up on supplies for college?" She bent down to bunch up her baggy socks. "What school are you going to?"

"Georgetown," Brenda said. "Part-time — so I can still counsel at Garfield House." Amy knew Brenda had been working at the Georgetown halfway house for over a year. "But that's not why I'm invading Ross's," she said. Brenda's gaze wandered to a jar of pens that were on sale. She reached over and grabbed a handful. Then she turned back to Amy and Colin. "Some of the kids at Garfield are really getting geared up to start the school year off right." Brenda grinned. "I'm their supplier." She flipped through a stack of specially reduced notebooks. "The kids *really* would be in great shape," she continued, "if they knew how to study. A couple of them are in remedial classes, and they have a hard time keeping up."

"Hey," Colin began, suddenly excited.

Amy glanced at him. One look at his face, and she knew he was going to tell Brenda about the Freedom Reader Workshop. She felt ridiculous, but she couldn't suppress the feeling of jealousy

13

she got when Colin talked about something that didn't include her at all.

She was being crazy again. She knew that. Why *shouldn't* Colin talk about his workshop? He was excited about it.

Amy leaned against Colin. What an idiot she was. Her confidence quotient was slipping again and for no reason at all. Why did she need constant reassurance from Colin? She knew he loved her. And why didn't realizing that make her *stop*?

Colin slipped his hand from hers and began surveying the posterboard situation again.

"So," Brenda said, eventually, "when is this magic workshop?"

"Next Friday night," Colin answered. He was talking to Amy now, too. She'd started thumbing through art books and was pretending to read.

Amy gulped. "Friday?"

Colin looked at her uncertainly and nodded. "Is something wrong with that?" He glanced at Brenda — she seemed puzzled by Amy's sudden outburst, too. "Everything works out great this way," he explained. "When you come home next Sunday, we'll be able to spend every minute together. No meetings in the way. No workshop." He kissed the tip of Amy's nose. His face shone so radiantly, she had to smile.

"How long does the workshop run?" Brenda asked.

"Friday night, all day and early evening Saturday. Then Sunday till noon."

"Well, I'll be there," Brenda promised. Her face brightened with honest anticipation. "This is something the kids at Garfield will really benefit from."

"Yeah," Colin laughed. "And if you're lucky, they won't give you as hard a time as the infamous Susan Atkinson gave *her* tutor!"

Amy chuckled, remembering how Susan had developed a major crush on Colin when he was helping her in math last spring. Luckily, Susan had met Colin's younger brother just when Amy and Colin were going to confront her with the news that they were in love.

Brenda asked Colin a few more questions about the workshop as they paid for their purchases and headed for the door. The idea of Colin being without her for three days didn't exactly thrill Amy, even though she knew she was being totally unreasonable.

Determinedly, she straightened her shoulders. That was it. She was centering the pendulum. No more of this insecurity nonsense. But she had a hunch her mind wasn't done with her yet.

Chapter
3

"Amy, get up! Mom's not taking us to Elk Springs. She's got a meeting in D.C. tonight, so she'll be driving up tomorrow. We have to take the twelve-thirty bus. And Colin called. He — "

"Hey! Wait a minute!" Amy rasped. "Give me a chance to regain consciousness, would you?" She burrowed her face under her pillow and scrunched the softness around her ears.

"A-my!" Susan persisted.

Amy sat up and swung her legs over the side of her bed. Still in a sleepy fog, she stretched her arms lazily over her head. Finally she stood up and wandered slowly down the hall to the bathroom. She paused when she passed by Susan's room. Rubbing her eyes, she stood in the doorway and looked around the room, then threw herself onto her sister's bed, laughing.

Tight-lipped, Susan glanced around, too.

"Okay, Miss Cheerful," she said sternly. "What are you laughing at?"

Amy propped herself on one elbow. "Can't you see?" A sweep of her arm took in Susan's bureau, desk, chair, and closet.

"See what?" Susan asked, her thumbs hooked in the pockets of her cropped white pants.

"You look like you're packing for a year," Amy declared. "Not just a weekend."

Susan's closet was nearly empty and her clothes were strewn all over the place. "Andrea's wedding is important to me," Susan said adamantly. "I want to look right."

Amy stood up and gave her sister a hug. "You always look right," she said, giving Susan's blonde ponytail a gentle tug. "Even after a sweaty game of tennis with that boyfriend of yours."

Susan aimed her nose at the ceiling. She issued a fake sniff. "I never sweat," she announced. "But anyway, big sister. I noticed *your* suitcase is all neatly packed already."

"So?" Amy stated.

"Well, if you ask me, no self-respecting teenage girl should be able to pack for a wedding in ten minutes."

"It really wasn't that hard," Amy teased, heading for the bathroom. Susan tagged along. "First of all, I don't have nearly as many clothes as you do, so I didn't have that many choices." She turned and put both hands on Susan's shoulders. "Nobody," she said in mock seriousness, "has as many clothes as you do. Besides," she added, uncapping the toothpaste, "in between racing

17

around with Colin this week, putting up posters, and getting Sam's foot rechecked, I had time to think about what I wanted to take."

"Whoops," Susan said, looking guiltily at Amy.

"Suze?" Amy said. "What's wrong?"

"Colin called," she said. "That's what I was trying to tell you while you were hiding under your pillow. He wanted you to call as soon as you got up." Susan smiled shyly. "He said something about this being your lucky day."

The hint of a smile touched Amy's lips, and she felt a surge of warmth spread through her. What a wonderful message to wake up to. Forgetting her shower, she headed for the phone in her mother's bedroom. She was still grinning as she dialed Colin's number. Busy. She would take a shower, then try again.

A few minutes later, she stepped out of the shower and smoothed baby oil all over her body. She rubbed it in with a soft striped towel and then ran back to her mother's room.

Colin picked up on the fourth ring. "Is this my lucky lady?"

"How'd you know it was me?" Amy teased.

"Magic," Colin whispered. His soft voice sent tingles shooting through her.

"So, why am I so lucky? Are you going to smother me with kisses on the way to the bus stop? Take my breath away?"

"I was thinking more along the lines of buying you an omelet," Colin quipped. "Not suffocating you."

Amy's stomach rumbled at just that moment,

and she realized she was starving. "Cheese with mushrooms?" she said.

"Cheese with mushrooms."

"At The Left Bank?"

"At The Left Bank. And stop with the questions already. I'm starving."

"Me, too." Amy looked at the art deco clock on her mother's bureau. It was ten o'clock. "Pick me up in half an hour. You can crush me with kisses on Sunday. Deal?"

"Deal. I'll see you soon."

Amy returned the receiver gently to its place, then sighed happily, and skipped down the hall to her sun-filled room. She felt so happy she thought her feet might leave the ground. Last week, in the art supply store, she'd felt uneasy about leaving Colin for three days, but the weekend would zoom by — she just knew it. She'd have a great time at Andrea's wedding. Colin would love his workshop. And that would be it: No moods, and no craziness. In fact, the separation should be good for them. By Monday morning, they'd be more of a couple than ever!

She lay back down on her bed, letting herself sink into a reverie, imagining Colin's greeting when she came home on Sunday. Sam hobbled in and nuzzled her hand. Pulling him onto her lap, she hugged him hard. He yelped and wiggled away from her.

"Cruel person," Susan teased. She entered holding a bowl of cereal. "Taking out your happiness on a poor, injured dog."

Amy made a face, then reached to give Sam a quick pat.

"How long have you got before Colin picks you up?" Susan said. She wiped a drop of milk from the corner of her mouth.

Amy checked the clock again. "Twenty minutes."

Susan frowned. "I wanted to get your advice on a dress I just finished making. I can't decide whether or not to take it."

Amy bent over and let her hair fall forward. Then she straightened up and peered at her sister between the damp strands. "I've got to dry my hair and get dressed, Suze."

Disappointment washed across Susan's face.

"Hey, come on," Amy said gently. "*All* your clothes are gorgeous. You haven't made a dress yet that I didn't like." She beamed at her sister. Susan had recently started designing and sewing her own clothes, and she had an incredible talent for it. And not only did it ease their mother's post-divorce money crunch, but it kept Susan looking her usual stylish self.

"Well, you never know who you might meet at a wedding," Susan said. "I just want to look my best." She held the royal blue cotton halter dress to her chest and swirled around with it, smiling into the mirror. "Maybe there'll be some cute boys there."

"Susan!" Amy wore a look of disgust. "You've *got* a boyfriend!"

"So?" Susan said. "I just want to have a good time. Besides, it can't hurt just *looking* at adorable guys. What's wrong with that?"

"You're impossible!" Amy groaned. She threatened Susan with a pillow, then said in a stern voice, "Now pack up. Then clean up, before Mom grounds you for a year."

In the bathroom, drying her hair, Amy's spirits sank a little. She'd figured out why by the time she'd smoothed on her blush and applied her lip gloss. It was Susan's remark about cute boys that worried her. But why? She wasn't like Susan. She wasn't even *thinking* about meeting someone at Andrea's. So what was the problem?

Placing her hands on her hips, she stood back, and stared at herself in the full-length bathroom mirror. Who was she trying to kid? She knew what the problem was. She loved Colin, but she just couldn't get herself to believe that *he* felt as strongly as she did. He didn't seem nearly as bothered as she was by the fact that they were about to spend three whole days apart. What if Colin were thinking the same thing Susan was — that this is his golden opportunity to meet some beautiful girls?

Amy felt herself tense. She hated being like this. It was as if she didn't know herself anymore. *Stop it*! she told herself emphatically. She *wouldn't* be like this. She didn't have to be if she didn't want to.

"Amy?" Susan banged on the door. "You've been in there forever. Are you almost done? I want to take a shower."

Colin gripped the steering wheel so hard his knuckles turned white. He let his foot sink a little harder on the accelerator. Ahead of him, the

21

road shimmered with heat. It seemed hours since he'd hung up the phone after talking to Amy, and he couldn't wait to see her.

He reached up to massage a tight muscle in his neck. Why couldn't he tell her how much he loved her? Surely Amy knew it, but why was he always so tongue-tied when it came to expressing his feelings? Why hadn't he said how much he was going to miss her, instead of going on and on about his workshop and dragging her around with him to put up posters?

Colin raked his hand through his hair. He adjusted the visor, then pushed the lever on the dash to maximum air-conditioning.

Maybe it wasn't the workshop that was making Amy act so distant lately. Maybe it was him. Maybe something about him was turning her off. What did he know about love anyhow? For years he'd been too shy to do anything more than think about it. And then he'd found Amy.

Sometimes when he held her in his arms and kissed her, studied her beautiful face, and lost himself in her cool blue eyes, he felt like they'd been together forever. She was so much a part of him now he could barely remember what his life had been like without her.

The air-conditioning blasted cold air on his perspiring skin, and he shivered. So many times he'd wanted to ask Amy if she was happy with him. But he was so afraid of what she would say. And besides, Amy seemed so sure of herself she'd think he was foolish for being so insecure.

Rolling down the window, he breathed in deeply. The air-conditioning blew cool air around his legs, while hot air from outside wafted in and settled around his neck and shoulders. It was thick with the scent of summer flowers.

Love, he thought glumly — it wasn't easy. Pulling in to the Atkinson driveway, he put the Bronco in park and turned off the ignition. He glanced up and saw Amy through the smudges in his windshield, waving at him from the doorway. He untangled himself from his seat belt and rushed from the car to where she was waiting.

His fingers trembled as he pulled her to him. He stroked her smooth, warm skin. Headily, he smelled the freshness of her.

No, he thought again, love *wasn't* easy. But loving Amy was better — much better — than anything else he'd ever dreamed of.

Chapter

4

The Left Bank Café was a little restaurant on the outskirts of Rose Hill. "It looks like someone transplanted this right out of Paris," Amy said with a sigh, glancing around the spacious sunlit room. "Yum!" Sighing with pleasure, she took another huge bite of her omelet. "And *you* brought me here," she whispered in Colin's ear, leaning across the square oak table to give him a kiss.

"Stop. Stop! Let me eat!" Colin teased, returning her kiss willingly. When Amy was settled back in her seat, Colin picked up the remaining half of his almond croissant and slathered it with butter.

"Uh-oh," Amy said, looking up from her omelet to check the wall clock. "It's eleven-thirty already."

Amy was surprised at herself. For months, she'd been wildly anticipating Andrea's wedding.

Now that it was here, part of her balked at the thought of leaving.

"Amy?" Colin looked concerned. "What is it?" he asked.

For a moment she clung to him across the table as if she never wanted to let him go. Then she pulled away. "Nothing," she answered. Amy tried to look calm, to seem as if she hadn't made a fool of herself. While Colin stared at her, she pushed around a slice of mushroom with her fork.

Colin put down his croissant. "Come on," he coaxed. Gently, he took hold of her hand. "We don't have that long before your bus leaves. If you won't tell me what's going on inside that head of yours, I'm going to kiss the truth out of you." He bent closer to her. "Right *here*."

A smile flickered across Amy's face. She was about to speak when a crumpled napkin bounced off her shoulder and dropped to her lap. She turned quickly and saw Brenda Austin and Dee Patterson waving from a booth a few tables away. Dee was a photographer for Kennedy High's school paper, *The Red and the Gold*. As usual, she had a camera by her side.

Colin angled his head toward the booth. "You up for going over there?" he asked.

Amy nodded. In spite of what she'd just been feeling, she wanted to talk to Brenda. She and Colin would be spending practically the whole weekend together, and Amy almost wanted to test Brenda out. It seemed ridiculous, but Brenda *had* just broken up with Brad . . . and she *was* in a vulnerable state. Oh, why was she always having these crazy thoughts? Amy knew Brenda was only a symbol of her fear of losing Colin. The real problem was *her*. Even so, her teeth clenched when she and Colin walked past the pastry counter and arrived at their booth.

"I thought you'd be in wedding-bell land by now," Brenda said, a teasing expression playing on her face. She cocked her head at Amy. "Where does your cousin live?"

"Elk Spring. It's about seventy miles from here."

"Oh, right," Brenda said. "It's one of those little towns with just one traffic light, isn't it?"

Amy nodded, and Dee took a sip of coffee. "What time's your bus?"

"Twelve-thirty," Amy answered. Then she pointed at the camera slung over the back of Dee's chair, and smiled. "Getting in a little practice for the wedding?"

Dee grinned broadly. "I still can't believe I'm playing 'real photographer' tomorrow."

Amy's eyes widened with surprise. "But you *are* a real photographer!" she declared. "You'll probably take better pictures than the professional." A local professional photographer would be at the wedding, but Andrea wanted Dee to take some candid shots. Dee had hit it off with the Moores in June when they came to visit the Atkinsons.

Brenda touched Dee's arm. "Tell them what else you'll be doing."

Dee just shrugged.

Colin shot her a playful look. "Come *on*."

"Well — " Dee spoke directly to Amy. "Let's just say that you and Susan better look gorgeous at the wedding."

Amy blushed. Then she tilted her head and frowned in confusion.

"Dee's going to be doing a photo feature for this year's first issue of *The Red and the Gold*," Brenda explained. "A four page spread on what a sampling of Kennedy kids have been doing this summer." Dee looked down at her plate modestly.

"That's great," Colin broke in. "Amy always looks gorgeous. She doesn't have to worry."

"Maybe Colin should drive up to Elk Spring tomorrow," Brenda teased slyly. She looked straight at Amy. "He'll probably go out of his mind being away from you for three days."

Colin threw his head back and laughed, pulling Amy to him tightly. She turned scarlet.

"Hey, Colin — " Dee said innocently. "Isn't there some kind of workshop this weekend?"

"Sure is," Colin said confidently. "And it's going to be great." He beamed at Brenda and disengaged himself from Amy to put a hand on Brenda's shoulder. "And," he added solemnly, "two of Kennedy's finest will be attending."

Amy felt her stomach turning flip-flops, and she excused herself to go to the rest room. "I'll be right back," she announced.

"Wow, she didn't look so great," Colin said with concern after Amy had left.

"I'll go see if she's okay," Brenda said, following Amy to the ladies' room.

As soon as she was gone, Dee scurried around

the table to where Colin was standing. She pulled out a chair and plunked him down on it. Gracefully, she slid into her own seat, next to him.

"Well — " she said. She clapped him good-naturedly on the back. "So you're going to be a swinging single this weekend."

Colin smiled weakly. "I'm going to be lonesome, you mean."

Dee looked surprised. "Even with your workshop coming up?"

Colin shook his head. "It's not the same, Dee. Sure, I'll be busy, but just knowing Amy's not around makes everything harder." He straightened up suddenly. "Hey, that reminds me. Do you have Andrea's number, Dee? I want to call Amy there tonight and surprise her."

"Sure. I have it at home. I'll call you with it later."

"Great," Colin said. He slid halfway down in his seat and said quietly, "Dee?"

"What's wrong, Colin?" she asked softly when she noticed his pained expression.

"Have you noticed anything different about Amy lately?" he asked haltingly. "She's been acting sort of strange, kind of distant. I'm not sure if it has anything to do with her parents' divorce, or — "

"Or what?" Her question was greeted with silence. "Colin!" Dee grabbed both his hands and clasped them tightly on top of the table. "Or *what*?"

"Listen," Colin began. "I don't want to sound like an idiot or anything — "

"You're *not* an idiot." Dee leaned toward him

intently. "Will you please tell me what you're talking about?"

Colin hesitated. When he spoke, his words came out painfully slowly. "Just between you and me and this croissant here," he said, fingering the pastry and managing a limp smile, "I'm not sure how Amy feels about me anymore."

Dee rolled her eyes, but shook her head sympathetically. "With all due respect, Colin Edwards," she said, "I think you're out of your mind!" She kept a firm grip on his hands. "I shouldn't be telling you this," she declared, "but Amy *adores* you! Are you listening, Colin?" Dee let go of his hands and put one hand on either side of his head, forcing him to look at her. "She *adores* you."

"Well!" Brenda peered over the table. Amy stepped up right behind her. "We leave for one minute," Brenda said, "and look what happens." Sitting down, she cast Amy a look of mock disgust. Solidly, she placed one hand on Dee's shoulder. "Tell me honestly," she said, with pretend mournful eyes. "Does this mean that you and Amy can't be friends anymore?"

Dee rolled her eyes and flopped back in her seat.

Amy grinned. She was fizzing with good feelings again. Every comment, every look, blew her in a different direction.

"Let's go," Dee said to Colin. She pouted like an insulted child. "Brenda and Amy don't love us anymore."

"Sit still," Amy said, laughing. "Don't think I'm going to let you two get away with this."

29

"Hey, Colin," Dee said suddenly. "Really. Do you have time for me to take your picture?"

She was already pulling the case off her Nikon. "I'm going to be missing a lot of the workshop because of the wedding," she explained, "and since you're one of the three stars responsible — Oh, c'mon," she urged. She left the camera case and lens cap on the chair. Insistently, she yanked Colin to his feet and tugged him toward the front door. "The bus stop's only a few minutes from here. This won't take long."

Colin shrugged helplessly as Dee dragged him through the restaurant. In a moment they were out on the sidewalk. Dee was snapping away.

Brenda laughed and shook her head. "That girl amazes me sometimes."

"Why?" Amy asked.

Brenda brushed croissant crumbs off the long Indian print skirt she was wearing. "Well, I just can't get over how much she's changed in the past half year — and I don't just mean physically. Since she lost all that weight, nothing can stop her. She seems so confident."

Amy nodded thoughtfully, thinking how her own confidence had taken a nose dive. She was so lost in her thoughts, she didn't notice that Brenda was sitting back in her seat, studying her intently. "Are you okay, Ame?" she asked.

Amy gave a little shrug. "Sure. Why?"

"I don't know. You seem — well, I guess you seem a little uneasy."

Amy toyed with a napkin.

"Is there something I can do?" Brenda coaxed. Her smile was warm and real.

"Don't worry about me. Really. I've got some stuff I have to work out in my head. That's all."

Brenda nodded understandingly. Her gaze wandered around the café. She quickly grabbed Amy's arm and pointed at the nearest window. Amy shook her head with a laugh.

Colin was outside waving in Amy's direction, trying to get her to smile. He had pirated Dee's camera and was clicking picture after picture of her seated at the table. By the time Dee managed to recover her Nikon, Colin had taken nearly half a roll of film.

Amy rolled her eyes at Brenda. She slid out of her seat and bolted for the door. "Have a great weekend!" Brenda shouted after her. With every step, Amy felt lighter and lighter, as if it would be the simplest task on earth to *fly* to Elk Spring.

Once outside, stumbling, giggling, running to the car with Colin, her hand safe in his, she thrilled to the feeling of being in love.

Chapter
5

Susan stuck her head out of the bus, her fingers gripping the top of the half-opened window. "Amy! Will you come *on*?! Mom didn't rush to get me here just so you could make us ten years late!" She shook her head impatiently, and her voice dissolved into grumbles. "We're not going around the world, you know. You'll see Colin the day after tomorrow!"

"Okay! Okay!" Amy called over the bus's thrumming engine. But she couldn't tear her eyes away from Colin's face.

So many times, she'd pictured their first real good-bye. This was the moment Colin was supposed to tell her how much he loved her, the moment he would sweep her into his arms and swear he didn't know how he'd get through the days without her.

That's sick, she chided. *Sick!* Where had all these romantic notions *come* from? Did they multiply inside her for seventeen years, waiting to spring out at the first unsuspecting boy she fell in love with?

In desperation, she took a deep breath and tried to muster some dignity. She smiled at Colin as he unlocked the back of the car and pulled out her suitcase. His blue eyes twinkled. "I guess this is it," she said.

"Not quite," he said, making his way around to the passenger side.

Amy's heart pounded when Colin produced a box from the glove compartment and handed it to her. She carefully tore off the shiny silver paper. "Oh, Colin. It's beautiful," she murmured. She slipped her necklace into the pocket of her skirt and replaced it with her new silk scarf.

"Something blue," Colin whispered, fingering the soft silk. "For *our* wedding." He looked at her with a shy, lopsided grin, and in that moment Amy thought she would burst with joy. "Whenever that time comes." His hands played slowly up and down her back, then lingered at her waist. "Miss me?" he asked suddenly, drawing her closer to him.

She swelled with feeling. "Oh, yes, Colin. I — " He stopped her words with a burning kiss. Then he pulled away.

"You'd better go," he said huskily.

Amy bent to pick up her suitcase. She backed slowly toward the waiting bus, practically in a trance from Colin's kiss and his sweet words.

A squeal of brakes snapped her out of her reverie. Brenda's Jeep careened to a stop next to Colin's Bronco, leaving a spray of gravel in its wake. Brenda leaped from the Jeep triumphantly, as if she'd just won an Olympic race. "Your purse!" she rasped breathlessly. She ran over and tucked a black clutch under Amy's arm. "It got mixed in with our stuff."

"Oh, Brenda, thanks," Amy breathed. "You saved my life!"

On the bus, she turned for one last look at Colin. Susan leaned over and looked out, too. Brenda was standing next to Colin, near his car. Amy returned their wave and saw Brenda turn to Colin and laugh. The bus lurched onto the highway, and Amy was left with an uneasy, helpless feeling. Susan settled into her seat. Amy faced front again and a shiver of fear ran through her.

Susan peered at her. "Don't!" she said sternly.

"Don't what?" Amy's voice was light, but she knew she looked worried.

"Don't be a crazy person! *That's* what! Colin and Brenda are just friends."

"I know that!" Amy protested.

Susan ignored her. "The guy is nuts over you, Amy." She spoke in a steady, deliberate voice. "He and Brenda have the workshop in common now. That's all." She dug her chin into her chest and tightened her ponytail. "Colin isn't looking for someone new. Stop worrying."

Amy pressed her head against her seat. She touched the scarf Colin had given her. "I forgot to wish him good luck," she said flatly.

"So, you forgot," Susan snapped. She turned and grabbed Amy's shoulders. "You know," she said, giving them a good shake, "You're too serious. Love's supposed to feel *good* most of the

34

time. You're always looking so glum, no one would believe you're in love."

Susan pointed to a mileage sign they were passing. "Look," she said in a crisp voice. "We have sixty-five miles to go before we get to Elk Spring. I want to sleep fifty-five of them. For the last ten miles, I intend to freshen up. Will you wake me in time?"

Amy nodded. The worry had vanished. Now she just felt silly.

Susan sank into her seat. Her feet rested on the metal bar attached to the seat in front of her. "Amy," she said sleepily, "with your imagination, you should write for the soaps." Yawning, she snuggled sideways into her seat, facing the window. She tucked her legs under her and slipped her hands between her cheek and her seat.

Amy scowled slightly. "Don't you ever worry about Rich?"

Susan yawned again. "No, never." She giggled. "I used up all my worrying trying to get Colin. Remember?"

Amy grunted. "*Do* I!"

Susan opened her eyes and grinned. "Well, now he's your boyfriend, and I don't have anything to worry about. And neither do you."

"Will you look at that face!" Uncle Sid exclaimed. He pinched Amy's cheeks between his fingers and planted a noisy kiss on her forehead. "Isn't Amy the spitting image of Andrea when she was that age?" He turned Amy around so she faced the entire family.

"Daddy!" Andrea stifled a smile. She shook her

35

head disapprovingly, and her long mane of golden curls glimmered in the sunlight. Her fiancé, Phillip, stood next to the Moores' Toyota van. Laughing softly, he loaded the suitcases.

"Sid," Aunt May called out. "Save your facial reconstruction for the operating room, will you?" Uncle Sid looked crestfallen. Aunt May ruffled the few hairs he had left on the top of his head. Plume, the family poodle, leaped from her arms and barked.

The ride to the Moores' home was glorious. Amy stared out the window as Uncle Sid wound the Toyota through the gorgeous countryside. It was three o'clock before they turned into the familiar, long, curving driveway. Honeysuckle vines edged the narrow lane. Ahead, in a clearing surrounded by sculptured hedges, rose the Moores' gracious stone mansion.

Amy loved the house — not just because it looked like it belonged on the cover of *House and Garden* — but because she'd always felt so comfortable there. She liked to pretend it was her country castle, at least that's what she'd done when she was little. How many mornings had she clambered up the twisted limbs of the old oak in the backyard and surveyed her peaceable kingdom?

"What made you decide to have the wedding at home?" Amy asked her cousin. She reached deep into the ceramic apple jar for another of her Aunt May's famous oatmeal raisin cookies. Then she passed the jar around. The family was lounging in a breakfast nook off to the side of the huge country kitchen.

Andrea swallowed the last bite of her cookie, flounced backward onto a chintz cushion, and slung her arm around Phillip's shoulder. "This is the place where I've been the happiest." She planted a quick kiss on the tip of Phillip's nose. Then she beamed at him. "Till now, anyway."

Phillip was twenty-four, a little short, but solidly built. He had a wonderfully handsome face with dimples that made him look about fifteen. He was also a very nice guy. Amy was glad she liked him so much and that he and Andrea seemed so right for each other. They had a lot in common, but they each were very independent, too, and Amy knew they could get along very well without each other if they had to.

Amy wished she could feel that way about Colin. But just the thought of him not being part of her life scared her silly.

"Did you see the size of that tent out back?" Susan exclaimed when she and Amy were alone in the guest room. She tore off her white cotton jumpsuit. Standing in just her underwear, she cooled herself in front of the fan.

"Mmmm," Amy answered. She lay sprawled face down across the yellow chenille bedspread. After throwing herself there ten minutes ago, she hadn't budged an inch.

"And the *flowers!*" Susan went on. She groaned with enthusiasm. "Uncle Sid must have bought out a nursery! There are enough flowers for every

37

room in the house — as well as the tent, every table set up out back, even every bathroom."

"Susan?"

"What?" Susan had taken off her mother-of-pearl dangling earrings and let her hair down.

Amy rolled over, her eyes still closed. "You are crazed," she said. "What you need is a cool — "

"Shower!" Susan blurted.

Amy opened her eyes and caught a glimpse of Susan streaking for the bathroom. Amy leaped off the bed just as the lock clicked. "Oh, come on," she pleaded. "*I* was supposed to go first." She pressed one side of her mouth against the door so Susan could hear her. Susan was belting out a gloating song above the pounding water.

In two seconds, Amy was on the bed again, face down, surrendering to sleep. No thoughts battled in her brain. She felt calm. Rose Hill might as well have been a million miles away.

She woke at five. The bathroom door was open and Susan's towel hung over the tub. Except for the branches tapping on the window next to her, the room was still.

Amy leaped out of bed. She saw Susan's note then: "Dear Sleeping Beauty — It's four-thirty. I'm famished. Am going downstairs to grab a bite and see if Aunt May needs help. I set the alarm for five-fifteen. Didn't have the heart to wake you."

Amy felt for the alarm button and turned it off. On her way to the bathroom, she stared into the mirror over the bureau. Drinks in half an hour, and she looked like Medusa. What else had Andrea said? Dinner at the Inn at six-forty-five?

Then home by eight-thirty to rehearse and have dessert.

Amy shook her head. Maybe somewhere in there she'd find time to take a breath or two!

In a minute she was stripped and in the shower, treating her hair to protein shampoo and conditioner. Squeaky clean, she slid into the pale peach calf-length slip her mother had loaned her. Then she pulled out her print silk dress. She held the dress against her in front of the full-length mirror on the inside of the guest room door. Her towel circled her head like a turban. Hastily, she checked to see how wet it was. Dry enough to get dressed. She yanked off the towel and tossed it into the bathroom. Dark strands of damp hair fell onto her shoulders and forehead. She walked over to the window, wondering if any guests had arrived. She was just in time to see a beat-up silver Chevrolet pull into the wide circular driveway. It clanked and clattered. Then the driver got out, and Amy couldn't keep from gasping. He was simply gorgeous.

The boy stood for a moment, tucking the tails of his yellow oxford shirt into his jeans. His shirt-sleeves were rolled to the elbow, revealing tanned, muscular arms. Amy smiled. This boy was as different from Colin as night was from day.

She pressed her dress tightly against her. She was aware of the warmth spreading through her and flushed. She tried to force herself to turn away, to do something that would stop the blood from racing through her veins, making her whole body tingle. But she was rooted to the spot. Without warning, the boy looked up at her.

His ruddy, broad-featured face broke into the most bewitching smile she'd ever seen. It seemed to pierce her soul. Giddily she hid behind the lace curtain sashed against the window.

Who *was* he? He certainly wasn't dressed to go out to dinner, so he couldn't be one of the guests. Could he?

Amy felt her insides go fluttery as she peeked out from behind the curtain and peered down again. A dizzying wave of disappointment flowed through her, and she gripped the windowsill tightly.

The old silver car was still parked where she'd seen it last. But the boy with the bewitching smile was gone. She closed her eyes and told herself she had no right to feel so disappointed. She didn't even know him.

Chapter
6

"Well, hello! You're up!" Aunt May's face radiated excitement. Her fingers circled a crystal vase containing two birds of paradise. She bent over to kiss Amy's cheek. "Isn't everything gorgeous!" she exclaimed, her green eyes shining. Her circular beige linen skirt whirled as she gestured at the rooms branching out from the main hallway.

"Like a fairyland, Aunt May. I'm so sorry I wasn't down here to help you."

"Don't look so guilty." Aunt May gave a little wave as she spoke. "There are more caterers around here than guests," she said flippantly, not looking pleased. "Your uncle insisted on that. He said I deserved to have a good time at my only child's wedding. I guess he was right, but — " She put a finger to her lips and looked around for a place to put the flowers. "I don't know," she mumbled distractedly. "Sometimes I get this feeling about where things should go, so I run around changing everything." She angled the back of her hand to her mouth and whispered to Amy behind it. "You're uncle thinks I'm silly."

Amy hugged her aunt soundly. "Well, I think you're *terrific!*" Then, unable to stop herself, Amy let her eyes sweep the surrounding rooms for the handsome stranger. Every minute since she'd seen him, she'd been daydreaming about him. Every minute, that is, except for the ones she'd spent trying to wipe all thoughts of him from her mind.

"Have you seen anyone else yet?" Aunt May asked, breaking into her thoughts. She set the vase on the mahogany library table, then took Amy's hands and pulled her closer, pretending to examine her face. "Nope," she said. "I don't see lipstick smudges or pinch marks." She laughed gaily. "I'd say you were still in good shape!"

Uncle Sid zeroed in from nowhere, brandishing a cheese stick. "May!" he said, scowling slightly. He plucked a napkin from a passing caterer and dabbed at his lips after swallowing the hors d'oeuvre. "You're monopolizing my favorite niece."

Aunt May rolled her eyes at him. So did Amy. Before Amy could protest, Uncle Sid was dragging her off to meet Phillip's parents.

Her head was spinning with thoughts of that hunk of a guy, and Amy was afraid she wouldn't be able to concentrate on making small talk with strangers. Suddenly, she felt an overwhelming need to be rescued. Where were Andrea and Susan when she needed them?

The truth was — and she knew this — she

42

should probably be grateful to Uncle Sid. She was a lot safer having him lead her around than she would be if she sought out the stranger in the yellow shirt. Then she pictured his smile and suddenly being safe didn't matter. She scanned the room, searching for him. She realized she wanted nothing more than to cross his path.

The next half hour swept past in a blur of introductions. Phillip's parents seemed very pleasant. His mother was pretty and had Phillip's same dimples. Phillip's stepfather was tall and intense-looking with thick, dark, wavy hair. When Amy was introduced to him, she had the oddest feeling she'd seen him before.

She caught a glimpse of Andrea and used her eyes to flash a subtle S.O.S. Usually she enjoyed meeting new people. But tonight, and the rest of the weekend, there would be so many of them. She grew exhausted just thinking about it. When Andrea swept in for the rescue and they reached the main hallway, Amy collapsed, giggling with relief, into her cousin's arms.

"Where's Susan?" she asked, recovering.

"In the kitchen I think."

"Alone?" Amy's heart leaped mysteriously to her mouth. She knew what a flirt Susan was. Suppose her sister was in the kitchen with the boy with the soul-stirring smile at this very second? Amy felt so confused. *She* wanted to find him. Then again, she didn't want to find him. One moment Amy hoped he'd approach her. The next, she prayed he wouldn't even look in her direction.

Her mind spun. She felt more like a top than a person. And now Andrea was staring at her.

"Alone?" Andrea echoed, as if she'd missed something. "With all these people wandering around here?" She shook her head, looking confused. "Did you ever see so many people? I'm having the hardest time remembering the names of all of Phillip's relatives. Come to think of it, I'm not even sure what my name is anymore."

Amy grinned at her. "Well, tomorrow it'll be Mrs. Phillip B. Stanton."

"No, it won't," Andrea corrected. "I'm keeping my own name. Andrea Constance Moore."

"That's great!" Amy said emphatically.

"Thanks. I like my name," Andrea said, matter-of-factly. "And I'm proud of it. And I don't think I should have to get rid of it just because I'm getting married."

An amused expression spread across Amy's face. "Phillip isn't changing *his* name, is he?" Before Andrea could answer, she pulled away with a little jump. "Uh-oh," Andrea said, noticing her mother waving at her. "I think I'm being paged.

"By the way — " Andrea paused. Her fingers lingered on Amy's wrist. She eyed her cousin's wide-shouldered dress and reached back to touch Amy's hair where it fell, shimmering, to her shoulders. "You look beautiful!" she said, and dashed away.

Amy stood alone for a moment, mesmerized by the food, colors, and fragrances swirling around her. The early evening light filtered softly through the rooms, bathing everything in a golden glow.

She had an urge to explore the kitchen. She felt determined as she headed for it. Two caterers carrying silver trays passed her. Amy leaned for a closer look at the sizzling hors d'oeuvres. Instantly, she collided with a blond, preppy-looking boy just behind them.

"Oops! Sorry." Amy looked at the boy, startled. She put a hand on his arm to steady them both. "Hi. I'm Amy Atkinson. Are you one of the ushers?" she asked.

"Yup." He smiled slowly and looked her over. "You must be one of the resident bridesmaids."

Amy nodded. "That's right."

The boy's face brightened. "Oh — you're Susan's sister," he said. "My name's Jim Dunne." His eyes continued to roam over Amy until she felt like an insect under a microscope. "I'm a friend of Phillip's. I just met Todd, the other usher."

"Todd?"

"Yeah. Phillip's stepbrother." Jim's eyes flitted toward where a few of the guests were gathering in the foyer. Some of them were family Amy hadn't seen in years. "Listen," Jim said apologetically, "I've gotta go. Would you believe it?" He looked amused. "Your uncle's planning to take everyone to the Inn by horse and carriage."

"Everyone? There are twenty or thirty people here!"

"Maybe not everyone. Most of 'em, though."

"But the Inn's miles away!"

"That's ri-ight," Jim singsonged. "But your uncle says he's allowed time for it. Anyway — " He headed for the foyer. "I promised your aunt I'd help organize the exodus."

In a moment, Amy was standing nervously just

inside the kitchen doorway. Susan spotted her immediately in the thinning crowd of guests. "It's about time!" she sang out from a corner of the room. "We thought you were never getting up!"

We? Amy thought. She shut her eyes and drew in a deep breath, praying that her sister hadn't latched on to the mystical stranger like she had Colin.

"So what are you standing there for?" Susan called across the huge kitchen. "Come here. I want you to meet someone."

Amy felt her hands ball into tight little fists at her sides. Even before she opened her eyes — before Susan weaved between some guests and tugged her into the corner — she knew who it was that Susan wanted her to meet.

The boy's back was to her, but he turned around slowly when Susan brought her over. Amy felt her heart stop. In place of the yellow shirt and jeans, the stranger had on a light gray three-piece suit. But he still wore the same bewitching smile she'd seen from the window.

"Amy? I want you to meet Todd Stanton. Todd, this is my sister."

"Todd?" Amy exclaimed. Phillip's stepbrother?

"Okay, okay," Todd chuckled. "If you don't like my name, I'll change it!"

"No . . . I didn't mean . . . Oh, never mind," Amy said, laughing. She felt her face turn scarlet.

"You're even more beautiful when your hair's dry," Todd said then. His voice was rich and low. He smiled slowly, his eyes drilling so deeply into her, she almost forgot Susan was there. She stared down at her blue patent pumps, a pleased expression frozen on her face.

Suddenly, the light over the sink blinked on and off. Amy looked up and saw Jim Dunne with his hand on the dimmer. "We'd better head out," he called.

"Do you know him?" Amy asked when Susan waved.

Susan slid her blue eyes over her sister's face. "Hey," she said, grinning, "while you were doing all that serious sleeping, I had to talk to *some*body."

"Oh," Amy said, glancing at Todd, her cheeks burning more than ever.

Susan grinned at Amy, her eyes teasing.

"Todd wouldn't let me or Jim get a word in edgewise just now," Susan went on. "All he talked about was the gorgeous girl he'd seen in the upstairs window."

Susan glanced down self-consciously. After a few long strides, she was standing by Jim.

Amy was positive that the muscles in her legs had turned to jelly. She was standing upright by miracle alone, and if something didn't happen fast to save her, she'd be flat on her face in no time. She held onto the kitchen counter to steady herself.

What Todd Stanton had done to her in two minutes, no other boy — not even Colin — had done to her — *ever*. Being with Colin was like being warmed by a slow fire. Standing next to Todd, she felt engulfed by a blaze. All this and he hadn't even flirted with her! There would be no saving her if he did that! Out of the corner of her eye, she caught him looking at her. She sensed he was reading her every thought.

"Hey, Amy!" Susan called. "If you two don't want to walk to the Inn, you'd better be out front in five minutes!" Susan gave Todd a coy look. "You be good to my sister," she said.

When Susan and Jim left, the room was quiet. Amy felt her pulse soar. She and Todd were alone.

Amy looked at him. She laughed shyly, then she reached for a potato chip from the bowl on the breakfast table.

"When I saw you from the window," Amy began at last, "I thought you might be a delivery boy."

Todd seemed genuinely surprised. Then he grinned. "Why'd you think that?"

Amy shrugged. "Your car, I guess. And the way you were dressed."

Todd smiled at her and his deep brown eyes twinkled. "But I wasn't carrying anything."

"Ah-*ha*!" Amy thrust her forefinger into the empty space between them and nodded sharply. "My conclusion exactly!"

The feeling was beginning to return to her legs. But her face still felt like her own private sun had been beating down on it. Gathering courage, she took her first unwavering look into Todd's dark eyes. Instantly she wanted to dive into them.

Todd was more rugged looking than his father; wilder, too, but he had that same intense look about him. Amy wasn't sure she'd ever be able to take her eyes off of him. Suddenly, she felt an irresistible urge to run her fingers through his dark hair. She wondered what it would be like to kiss him. She refrained from touching him and followed him into the empty den and onto the couch. They didn't have much time to spend alone together before it was time to leave for the rehearsal dinner, but they could at least talk for a little bit.

"I *was* a delivery boy for a while," he said. "Before my father married Phillip's mother six years ago. My dad was a frustrated inventor then." He laughed. One side of his mouth lifted in a slow smile. "Then Dad got lucky. He and Phillip's mom started marketing some of his inventions." He raised his eyebrows and nodded. "Don't let her comfy look fool you." He looked at Amy. "Did you meet her?"

Amy nodded.

Todd let out a slow, admiring whistle. "That lady is some businesswoman!"

"So," Amy put in, "you're one big happy family."

Todd nodded thoughtfully. "Yeah, I guess so. Phillip thinks so much of my dad he took his name. And Dad's his best man tomorrow."

A prickly sensation gathered behind Amy's eyes as she thought of her own fractured family. She knew she'd cry if she didn't keep on talking.

"So," she asked lamely. "Why'd you come here incognito — in jeans?" She flashed Todd a nervous smile. "Were you out roping cows?"

"Close," Todd teased. His eyes sparkled. "I was on my way back from visiting a vet I know who lives around here — Dr. Victor. She's great."

Todd spoke excitedly. "She cares so much about the animals she takes care of." Todd looked sheepish then, as if he thought he sounded silly. "I'd give anything to work with her. Anyway," he said, "a calf was down — it had some kind of infection, and I was around at just the right time to help out. So I called Phillip. He made sure my clothes were brought over here."

"Do you want to be a vet?"

Todd released a hopeful whoosh of air. Then he nodded tentatively. "More than anything," he said.

"What year are you in?" she asked. She relaxed and sank back against the cushions. Todd shifted toward her slightly, and Amy thought her insides would melt. The closer he came to her, the more she seemed to be losing control.

"I'll be a sophomore," he said.

"What school?"

"Maryland."

"Does Maryland have a vet school?"

"Uh-uh. I'll be going to Penn if I can keep my grades up."

"You will," Amy said encouragingly. The world was perfect suddenly. But it would be even more perfect if Todd would take her in his arms and kiss her. Her heart pounded and she felt her cheeks grow warm. She realized she had never longed for anything so much.

Todd's eyes blazed, reflecting all she was feeling. His breath came faster then, and he reached out and traced her profile lightly with his finger. His hand came to rest just under her chin, and she let herself be drawn to him.

Hypnotized, she watched his lips part slightly, then closed her eyes as they met hers. Slowly, she slid her hands upward along his sides, then wound her arms around his neck and pulled him close. She was drowning then — drowning in his embrace, but she would have screamed if anyone had tried to save her.

Chapter
7

"Sssh," Susan said. She put her fingers to her lips, then pointed to the next table where Uncle Sid was on his feet, clinking his glass with his spoon, and gazing down on his daughter with shining eyes. Andrea and Phillip had just come into the Inn's lavish banquet room.

"Where have they been?" Amy whispered.

Susan tossed her a look, then whispered back. "Where would *you* be if you were them right now — filling your face or trying to spend a few minutes alone?"

The girls turned their attention back to their uncle who was waiting to speak.

"A toast!" he announced. He raised his champagne glass, and everyone in the room followed suit. Reflected candlelight flickered in fragile crystal globes around every table.

Phillip had his arm around Andrea as he nestled close and whispered in her ear. Amy watched her uncle watching and felt her lips tremble. She bit her lip, but that didn't stop the burning in her throat or the tears welling in her eyes.

"Andrea — " Uncle Sid continued. He gazed at her across the room. His voice broke, and Aunt May reached up and placed her hand on his arm. Uncle Sid gripped her shoulder and went on. "Once," he said softly, "you were such a little girl, and now — " He gave a little wave in her direction, then put down his glass, his gaze following his fingertips as they pressed into the damask tablecloth. When he looked up, his eyes brimmed with tears.

"I . . . I had a little speech prepared," he said haltingly, "but. . . ." Andrea rushed to his table and threw her arms around her father. She, too, had to squeeze back tears.

Uncle Sid looked so grateful and so proud of her — all at the same time — that Amy was close to tears, too. She wanted to look away, but her eyes were riveted to her uncle's face. She felt an explosion building inside her as her mind filled with images of her own father.

"Amy?"

Susan looked across the table at Amy and leaned fiercely away from Jim who'd put his arm around her shoulder. Amy reached across him and gripped Susan's hand.

"Never mind, dear," Aunt May was saying to Uncle Sid. Her glistening eyes swept over the rapt faces of her family and closest friends. "I think everyone understands what you're trying to say."

Amy's spirits rose when the toast was over, and

53

the room again swelled with the sounds of laughter, forks clanking against plates, ice tinkling in glasses. The musicians began tuning up again. Amy looked beyond them and found Todd. She'd seen him standing at the buffet, listening, during the toast. Now he was gazing warmly at her. She found she had to gasp for breath. She couldn't get over how much she was attracted to him.

She excused herself from the table and went to meet him at the side of the room. A little laugh escaped her, seeing the amount of food he'd collected. He headed toward the carrot-raisin salad, and her mouth dropped open. "You're really going to put something else on that plate?"

"A growing boy's gotta eat," he said. But he put down the serving spoon. His face lit up with a beaming, teasing smile.

"So where's *your* food?" Todd asked. He looked behind her. She laughed. Then he looked at her intently. "You okay?" He set his plate on the corner of the table and drew her into an alcove where no one could see them. "You're not eating," he said. He smoothed her hair off her forehead and encircled her face with his hands. "And before, when we got out of the carriage, you looked — " He hesitated, trying to find the words. "Well, beautiful, but a little, uh, spaced, too. And *then* you tore into the Inn like Cinderella trying to beat the clock."

Amy touched Todd's cheek. He looked so worried about her, but what could she tell him? That the wedding rituals were tearing her apart? Everything was so beautiful, so romantic. But thoughts of her father — of Colin — kept shooting up like geysers.

"We'll talk," Todd announced earnestly, as if that would fix everything. "I want to be with you."

Then his eyes gleamed devilishly. "But first — " He slipped his arms around her back and pulled her to his chest. "First — !" He dipped her. Amy squealed, then held her breath until he pulled her up and let her go.

"First *what*?" she said.

He wiggled his eyebrows and she giggled. "First," he said, "we *eat*!"

Amy stifled her laughter.

"I mean it!" Todd said. He grabbed her hand and dragged her into the banquet room. "I spent so much time talking back at the house — about *you*! — not one hors d'oeuvre touched my lips."

"Oh, come on." Amy gave him a disbelieving look. He flashed back an innocent one, but then his face turned serious. He stopped in his tracks and turned toward her. Amy found it hard to breathe when he brought his face close to hers. He traced her mouth lightly with his fingers. "All I could think about was you," he whispered. "But now I'm *starving*."

Amy laughed. Todd picked up his plate. He added a hunk of pumpernickel and headed for their table. Three steps later, he looked back at her. "Hurry up," he said engagingly. "There's not much left. And, anyway, I don't want to have to suffer too long without you."

She smiled at him. Amy had started to realize that she could never know what to expect from

Todd Stanton. She picked up a plate and hesitated over the chicken curry.

"What is *this*?" Uncle Sid came up beside her. "The new Don't-Eat-At-The-Wedding-Weight-Loss-Diet?"

"No!" she protested. "I just started."

"Good," he said. "Somebody's got to eat all this." He indicated the buffet with a sweep of his hand.

Amy grinned. She gave him a quick peck on the cheek, then pretended to be serious. "Don't worry, Uncle Sid." She heaped a generous portion of chicken curry on her plate. "I'll get fat for you. I promise."

"Oh, thank you, thank you," he said, straight-faced. He gave her chin a melodramatic squeeze. "You won't regret this."

By eight-thirty, the guests had gathered back at the Moores' house for dessert. The members of the wedding party had gathered in the sun room for the rehearsal. Amy stood back for a moment and marveled. The airy porch had become a chapel. Roses and gladioli exploded around the room with color. Cushioned chairs sat in seven neat rows facing the tiny altar. The pathway between them had been sectioned off with generous loops of pink satin ribbon. Slender white candles rose from several ceramic candelabras Aunt May had collected on her trips to Europe.

Amy closed her eyes. Then she opened them so the sight of the candlelight and flowers could sweep her away all over again. She sighed, not wanting to move, as if twitching one toe would make the magic go away.

Aunt May had engineered the transformation. The Moores' housekeeper, Mrs. Lindsay, had carried it out while everyone was at dinner.

"Gather round, everybody." The minister beamed happily from the front of the room. "There's dessert waiting for us, I've been told." His eyes teased playfully. "And I know how hungry you all are."

Aunt May flushed. She slipped her arm around Uncle Sid's pudgy waist and moved closer to him. Amy stayed put, still transfixed.

"Hello there." Todd whispered his words along the back of her neck. Her heart nearly stopped. She shivered and lifted her shoulders slightly, sure that everyone could see the color rising in her cheeks, hear the bells going off in her head.

She leaned into Todd, cherishing his nearness. A moment passed before she could make herself resist him. She tugged at his coat sleeve and started toward the front of the room. "Let's go," she murmured reluctantly. "We're going to miss something important if we don't get up there."

"Hey, wait a second." Todd reached for her and backed her against him. She giggled softly, hoping no one would turn around. "Did you hear?" he whispered. He ran his hands up her arm and cupped her shoulders. His lips nuzzled her neck.

"Mmmm?"

"The word's out that you're the girl I'll be walking back up the aisle with."

Amy turned to look at him. His words had slid

out so easily. She felt a sudden chill and explored his eyes. Was he playing with her? The sparks she'd been feeling — was he feeling them, too?

Colin's face rocketed through her mind at that instant, thrilling her strangely. It blocked out Todd's face. "Something blue," Colin had said, " — for when it's our turn." But now his face disappeared like a shooting star losing its light. It was Todd's face in front of her. Rose Hill was a universe away again. Amy let out a deep sigh. So this was how it felt, swinging between two worlds.

"Well?" Todd was staring at her. "Are you up for it?"

Amy shook her head to clear it. "Up for what?"

" 'The Long Walk,' " he teased, pronouncing the words slowly. "We'll be practicing it soon."

"I'm up for it," Amy answered, but her voice sounded hollow.

The rehearsal flew by. How she managed to tune out her confusion, Amy didn't know. She was just glad she could enjoy it.

"You're next," Aunt May said. She steered Todd and Amy toward their positions at the end of the aisle. "Don't trip!" she kidded.

The minister signaled and they took their first step together. Amy stiffened with excitement. Her body trembled as she marched in slow time to the imaginary music. She heard Todd breathing and matched her breath to his.

Was it fate that they'd found each other? Stranger things had happened.

She felt Todd's arm press against her own, and a flash of heat raged through her.

Chapter
8

Colin dashed in through the double doors that opened to the hallway beside the library. He checked his watch. Six-forty. "Oh, great," he groaned. The odds were two to one against him that the trainer was already inside — probably a lot of volunteers, too. And where had *he* been? Colin bulldogged around the corner of the library hallway, nearly slamming into Brenda Austin. He'd been slumped on a bench in the quad — that's where he'd been — watching a spider crawl across his shoe and mooning about Amy.

Brenda put a restraining hand on Colin's arm. "Easy!" she said. "This isn't a *speed*-reading workshop, is it?"

Colin rolled his eyes and held up his hand for mercy. He shook his head. "Please, counselor. No jokes." He pitched his thumb toward the library door. "Is she in there — are *they* in there?"

Brenda smirked. "Is *who* in there?"

"I don't know — the trainer, Marc, Dick, the volunteers — anybody!" Colin blanched, hearing the panic in his voice. The worry was understandable, though. He had organized the entire program. If it turned out to be a failure, he was the one responsible. Not Dick, not Marc. Not the trainer. *Him!*

Brenda took his hand. "Come with me, Mr. Nerves." She led him to the windowed library door. "Why don't you look for yourself?"

Colin peeked through the window. Marc and Dick were there talking with the trainer, Mrs. Gladstone. About fifteen volunteers had arrived.

Colin shook his head. "Geez. The trainer looks kind of stiff." He shoved his glasses up on his nose and glanced at Brenda. "I sure hope this goes all right. If that lady bombs tonight, the whole program gets deep-sixed." Colin started to push open the heavy swinging door.

"Hey, Edwards." Brenda's hand was on his shirt. She pulled him backward.

"What?" Colin let go of the door handle and looked at her.

Brenda locked glances with him. She spoke evenly. "Stop worrying. It's not going to bomb."

A slow smile crept up Colin's face. He took a deep breath and worked his fingers into his shoulders to relax his muscles. "It's not?"

"No way." Brenda looked incredibly excited. "It's going to be *great*!"

By six-fifty-five, the library was teeming with volunteers. Colin counted heads. When he got to thirty-five a huge grin spread across his face. He'd expected thirty people, tops.

Dick and Marc handed out materials while Mrs. Gladstone studied her notes. The volunteers began arranging the wooden chairs into a semicircle around the podium. Dee was there snapping picture after picture for *The Red and the Gold*.

Colin steadied himself. He could hardly believe it. This workshop was *not* a figment of his imagination. All the posters. All the planning. This night was really going to *happen*!

A few minutes after seven, Colin checked the hall for stragglers. When he came back, he approached Brenda from behind and put his hands on her shoulders. "Wish us luck," he whispered. Then he collapsed into a chair and pretended to wipe away a torrent of perspiration. "I'm glad Dick will be doing all the talking," he confessed. "I'd be a wreck by now."

Brenda looked at him with a puzzled smile. "You're kidding, Colin. I thought you'd love all that stuff — and be good at it, too. After all, you're going to be Kennedy's next student council president."

Colin reddened and tipped an imaginary hat. "I know, I know. I intend to practice up on my public speaking in the next couple of weeks."

Brenda laughed. "You're cutting it pretty close, aren't you?"

"Well, anyway, that's different," Colin insisted. "I can talk about politics and school government and all that. It's just talking about myself and a project that I organized that's so difficult."

"Well, I'm ready to get smart," Brenda said. She rummaged for a pencil and placed it, ready to use, near her open spiral notebook. "And I *do* wish you good luck," she said sincerely.

Colin smiled warmly at her. He waved to Dick. Dick got the go-ahead from Mrs. Gladstone. At once, he was on his feet. He stood behind the podium, facing a still-buzzing crowd.

Colin felt his own breath catch as Dick began speaking. So much rode on this first impression.

"You're all lucky," Dick began. His voice was powerful but friendly and struck just the right note of informality. "I hope you realize that." He cleared his throat. "There's a lady here tonight who's going to teach you something you don't know." A close-lipped grin broke straight across Dick's face. He paused for effect. "Just maybe," he went on, "some of you brain children are curious about what that could possibly be — " The audience laughed. "If that's the case, then listen up." Nobody seemed ready to concentrate yet, and Colin tensed. He jammed his hands into his pockets and looked at Brenda. She gave him a sympathetic smile.

"All right," Dick said after waiting a few moments for the audience to settle down, "you asked for it! I've got my bouncers Marc Harrison and Colin Edwards here. They're ready to take on anyone who doesn't pay attention."

The crowd hooted with pleasure. Colin half-stood and flexed his muscles. As if on cue, on the other side of the room Marc did the same.

Dick held up his palms for silence. "Mrs. Gladstone, here — " He gestured at the confident-looking, middle-aged woman. "Hey, wait a minute. Why don't I let *her* say it?"

The trainer eased herself from her seat and walked slowly and deliberately to the podium. When she settled herself behind it, she searched the faces in the crowd with a smile flickering on her face. The only sound was the whirring of the failing air-conditioner. "Since it's a weekend night," she said, "I know it wasn't mere curiosity that got all of you here." A few people tittered. "What I want you to do now," she said when they'd stopped, "is stand up and tell everyone what you expect to give to — and get from — this workshop."

No one got up, and Colin groaned inwardly. Half the kids in the workshop were there because they wanted something good on their college applications. The rest? He just hoped they'd have the dedication they needed to help the kids in the program.

Mrs. Gladstone didn't waver for a minute. It was almost as if she didn't want anyone to speak. Colin watched her closely. She looked confident to him, as if she had expected this resistance. Then she began speaking again. She told the group how important they would be to the children they tutored, how much they'd be helping to lower the illiteracy rate in the country.

Colin shook his head. That's what the trouble was — what everyone was afraid of — that they would blow it.

"Don't you see?" the trainer said forcefully. She swung in Colin's direction just as Brenda rose hesitantly from her seat to say something. "Just

63

a minute, dear," Mrs. Gladstone said. "I want to make a point here."

She nodded at her audience. "How were you feeling just now?" she asked. "Were you feeling smart — all you bright young people with good grades?" No one answered. "You weren't?" she said. "Why? Because you were embarrassed, right? Because you couldn't perform?" She paused for a sip of water, then came around to the front of the podium. "I'd bet that each of you is pretty confident in at least one thing that you do, something that you do very well, or some system you've worked out to get over the rough spots. Am I right?" She raised her eyebrows and waited.

"Right!" a boy exclaimed. Other volunteers echoed him.

"Well, people who can't read feel they'll *never* be able to perform, that they'll never be able to get over the rough spots. Do you get the picture?"

Colin nodded along with everyone else. Relief flooded through him as if a dam had broken. Not only were *other* people starting to enjoy the workshop, *he* was enjoying it. He glanced over at Marc and saw that Dee had stayed. She'd pulled her chair close to Marc and was listening intently.

"Now," the trainer said, "before I say anything more, I'd like to let this patient girl over here speak her mind." Mrs. Gladstone issued Brenda an encouraging smile, then leaned back, giving her the floor.

"I think everything you've said so far is true," Brenda began. She looked at Mrs. Gladstone and took a deep breath, then went on in a surer, louder voice. "But I'm not an expert tutor. What if I do harm to someone who really needs help? What if I turn them off reading permanently? What if the kids I tutor end up worse off then they were before I tried to help them?" Brenda's voice quavered. Colin thought that she suddenly looked like a small, innocent child. "I don't think I could take that. I really don't." She sat down quickly. Colin tapped her on the shoulder, and she turned sideways in her chair to look at him.

"You can't ruin them," Mrs. Gladstone answered in a strong, even voice, her eyes sweeping past Brenda to include the entire audience. Her eyes sparkled with enthusiasm. "If you were a youngster who didn't think you were very smart, what could be greater than having someone tutor you, someone who wasn't spending time with you for money? Someone who is spending time with you because they want to, because they care. Just your being there, caring, more than makes up for imperfect techniques. And caring goes a long way toward helping people realize just how smart they really are. Everyone got it?" The room exploded with cheers and applause. Mrs. Gladstone stood smiling, with her hands on her broad hips. "Good," she said. "Now, does anyone else have anything to say?" No one did. Mrs. Gladstone rolled up her sleeves. "Okay, then," she announced. "Let's get started."

Brenda had almost reached her Jeep in the school parking lot when Colin caught up with her.

"Slow down!" he called out. She looked confused for an instant, as if she didn't recognize him. Then he paused under a street lamp, and she grinned at him. After the community of the workshop, Colin didn't want to be alone.

Brenda held the key to her prized car in her hand. She had gotten the Jeep as a graduation present, and she'd certainly need it in the coming year for her commute back and forth to Georgetown and to Garfield House.

"It's a little late to be jogging, wouldn't you say, Fearless Workshop Leader?"

"Too late for compliments, too?" Colin ventured.

"Never!" Brenda leaned her elbow against her Jeep.

Colin rested his foot on the Jeep's back fender. "I just wanted to tell you how great I thought you were in there. What you did took a lot of guts — "

"Standing up to speak?"

"Yeah, that, but mainly the way you said what you were feeling. Do you know how much easier you made it for all the cowards in the room? For *me*, for instance. Your doing that really made me take a good look at myself."

"Aren't you making too much of all this?"

Colin put his hand up. "Let me finish, okay?" He hesitated and looked down at the ground, then shuffled from one foot to the other.

"Sometimes," he said haltingly, "when I'm with Amy" — he reached down to rub a nonexistent smudge off his topsider — "I have an awful time telling her what I'm feeling."

Brenda touched his arm.

"Believe me, Brenda. The way you can open up . . . it's a gift."

66

Brenda waved him off. Her baggy purple pull-over caught on the door handle.

"A gift that should be rewarded," Colin went on. A silly grin spread over his face.

Brenda smiled back at him, and disengaged herself from the car door. "Rewarded with what?"

"Oh, just the biggest steak sub Rose Hill has to offer. With double the onions and hot peppers."

Brenda laughed and held her nose. "I don't know. . . ."

Colin stood back, his arms flared open. "Why not?" he said innocently. He swiveled to look behind him. "We're dateless. No one to offend with our bad breath!" Brenda grimaced and shook her head. "Definitely, tragically so. There's only one problem," she said. "I'm not that hungry."

"I'm not, either," Colin admitted. He hesitated. "French fries?"

Brenda grinned. "French fries."

"Great. Five minutes." Colin started off. Brenda opened her door and climbed in.

"Wait!" In one stride, Colin was back at her window. "I can't stay out too late. I have to call Amy."

Brenda threw him a teasing look. "Have to?"

"*Want* to," Colin said, rolling his eyes. He pretended to reel. "Whew! Do I!"

"No problem," Brenda told him. "I promised Chris we would have a pow-wow about our college wardrobes. We've worked it out pretty fairly, I think," she said with a straight face. "I get fifteen minutes of consultation time. Chris gets eight hours."

Chapter
9

"Amy! Do you believe this?!" Susan glared down at the side zipper of her bridesmaid dress. It had just taken a nip out of her waist when she tried to close it. "Did I eat *that* much tonight?" The look on her face dared Amy to say yes. The two of them had decided to try on their dresses one last time before the big day.

"Sssh!" Amy stifled a giggle. She ran to the guest room door and closed it tightly. Her own pink silk taffeta dress was draped over her arm, ready to be tried on. She sauntered back to the bureau and sat down in a chair beside it. "Now let's see," she said. She stroked her chin, then broke into a pseudo-French accent. "Eet ees true you deed not try on zees dress before dinner, so we have no measure of zee time in wheeech you got so fat!"

"Amy!"

Amy held up her hand for silence, her face

deadpan. "But eef I remember correctly your level of food consumption zees evening" — She rubbed her temples slowly, and closed her eyes — "you ate — "

"Watch it!" Susan warned, grabbing her bed pillow and taking aim.

Amy laid her dress on the bed. " — Like zee peeeg!" she burst out, holding up her arms to ward off the pillow. "Easy!" she shouted as Susan launched her second attack. "You'll tear your dress."

She pushed Susan aside and jumped to her feet. "Come on. Let me see," she said, panting slightly. "Maybe you got a thread caught."

She bent down to get a closer look at Susan's zipper and sure enough, a wiggly thread was snagged between two zipper teeth. Carefully, Amy worked it out. Then the zipper slid up easily, as if it had been slicked with oil.

Susan retrieved Amy's dress. "Your turn," she said, handing it to her, "and hurry up. Aunt May wants us downstairs for dessert."

Calm again, Amy leaned wistfully against the bureau. "Suze, do you think my wedding will be as beautiful as Andrea's?"

Susan was slipping into her dinner dress again. "Sure it will" — she paused for effect — "But who do you think you'll marry — Colin or Todd?"

Amy bristled. "That's a pretty rotten thing to say."

Susan loosened her belt a notch and examined her reflection in the mirror. She jutted out her lower lip and shrugged. Her expression was half serious now. "It just seems to me," she said, "that for someone who made such a big deal about loyalty before we came up here, you're acting a little weird."

Amy's mouth flew open. "What about you and Jim Dunne?" she accused. "He's been running after you all night."

"That's right," Susan said brusquely. "But the difference is, I don't want him to."

Tears welled up in Amy's eyes. "So *I'm* the bad guy — "

Susan sighed. She eased a comforting arm around Amy's shoulder. "No, you're not," she said. "I'm sorry. I didn't mean to make you feel bad."

Amy managed a small smile, but her body was stiff with tension.

Susan sat down on the bed and sighed. "The truth is I don't know what I would have done if Jim had turned out to be a different kind of person — as nice as Todd, for example." She smiled wryly. "I could tell myself how strong I'm being — how loyal to Rich — because I'm trying to keep Jim away from me." Susan giggled. "But really I'm doing it for myself."

Amy tried to muster a smile but her lower lip began to tremble. "Colin would feel awful if he knew how I was feeling."

Susan nodded reluctantly. "You know," she said, putting great thought into her words, "If someone as great as Todd was crazy about me, I'd probably have told him I couldn't live without him — and that would be just for *starters*."

Amy let out a small laugh but she still felt

miserable. How could she betray Colin so easily?

"It's true. I'm not as nice as you when it comes to guys. I fall in love too easily." Susan said.

"And I don't?"

"It's not the same thing." Susan reached down to smooth her textured panty hose. "You may seem like the Bendict Arnold here, but you're not. You feel more guilty about this Todd business than I would have."

Amy made a face. "Oh, wonderful," she said. "Then I'm not a *complete* criminal."

"Right," Susan replied cheerfully, her eyes flying to the clock. She shifted gears. "Now, please, hurry up."

Amy eased the pink taffeta dress over her head. She groaned pitifully. Unbelievable. Two seams had ripped slightly since the last time she'd tried it on. Is this how life was going to treat her now because she'd fallen head over heels for Todd Stanton?

"Don't panic," Susan said, seeing the ripped seams. She rummaged through her night table drawer and found her travel sewing kit. Amy held her arms out to either side and Susan started pinning. She was only half finished when she ran out of pins. She again checked in her kit and wrinkled her nose in disgust. "Terrific," she grumbled. "I don't even have the right color thread."

Amy clasped her hands behind her neck. "What now?" she asked wearily.

Susan swirled a finger in front of her face. "Never fear," she said. "I'll be right back."

"Hurry," Amy called after her, but Susan had

already shut the door. Her heels clicked down the stairs.

When Todd knocked on the door and walked into the room a moment later, Amy sagged with disbelief. She was sure she'd never looked worse.

She didn't want to put her arms down, because of the pins. Her hair looked like a bird's nest. An abandoned scarecrow would have been more appealing. All this — plus Todd standing in front of her — made her face blaze red. "What are you doing here?" she asked.

"Hey, thanks a lot!" Todd made tickling motions with his hands, which came threateningly close, and Amy squealed. "Be good," he said, "or I won't let you have any eclairs or Napoleons or cheesecake — "

"Cheesecake?" Amy's eyes lit up.

"Uh-huh." Todd smiled. "Oh, I almost forgot. You have a phone call." A quiet drumming began in Amy's heart. "Jim told whoever it was to hold on — that you'd take the call in your room." Todd glanced at the phone. It sat on the night table between the two beds. "It didn't ring?"

"Uh-uh. It's been broken since April." Amy looked from one outstretched arm to the other and smiled sheepishly. "Can you pick up for me? I've gotta figure out how to move around in this get-up."

Todd shrugged. "Sure." He kneeled on the bed and stretched over to reach the receiver.

Suddenly, Amy realized that it was probably Colin calling. What had she been thinking? How could she have let Todd answer? Too late.

"Hello?" Todd said. Amy's breath stopped. She fiddled with some pins. Maybe it was her mother on the other end. Maybe. . . .

Todd clapped his hand over the mouthpiece. "It's some guy," he said.

"Some guy?" Amy's voice rose three octaves. Todd's eyes were fixed on her face.

"Here." He held out the phone. Amy wished he'd asked her if she wanted to talk. Pins pricked her side as she walked around the bed to the night table.

"Amy?" Colin's voice sounded deep and flat and far away. Visions of Rose Hill flashed through Amy's mind. Her garden. Sam. Her room. Colin's face.

Todd was no more than a ghost to her now. She pretended he wasn't sitting on the bed next to where she stood. As if reading her mind, he got up and moved to the window. Amy walked around Susan's bed, stretching the phone cord until she was next to the guest room door and far away from him.

"Colin," she whispered. She tried to keep her confusion out of her voice. She spoke with her back to Todd, curling the phone cord nervously with her fingers. "How did you get my number?" she asked. "And how are you?"

"I'm fine," Colin said. "Dee gave me the number. How about you? You okay, too?"

"Uh-huh." She hesitated. "Has your reading improved?"

Colin laughed. The sound was so sweet, so familiar. Visions of all her good times with him came flooding back fiercely. She squeezed her eyes shut. For a moment, neither of them spoke.

"Amy?" Colin said then. "Who answered the phone?" He paused. "Andrea's fiancé?"

Amy's hands were shaking. Colin sounded so hopeful. She would rather hurt herself than even think of hurting him, but what could she say? Should she lie to protect him? Would that be kinder than telling the truth? If only she had more time to think —

"It wasn't her fiancé," she answered finally.

"Was it one of the ushers?" Colin's voice wavered slightly.

"Yes."

"Is he still there?"

"Uh-huh." Amy tried to sound casual. "Why?" she blurted out and was immediately sorry. She knew perfectly well *why* he wanted to know. There was a moment of awkward silence. She was dizzy, feeling Colin's pain. The fan was whirring, but the steamy August night seemed suddenly hotter.

"Uh . . . I don't know," Colin said. "So, are you having fun up there?"

"I guess," Amy rang out nervously. "What about you? Is that trainer of yours as good as you hoped she'd be?"

"She's great," Colin answered. "Amy?" He hesitated. She felt as if an avalanche were crushing her, smothering her every breath. "You still coming home on Sunday?"

"Yup. Right on schedule." It was becoming increasingly difficult for her to talk. She was suddenly intensely aware of Todd standing across the room from her. She knew her voice would break, give away her feelings, if she didn't get off the phone soon. She closed her eyes. Her body tensed. "Colin," she said, her voice urgent, "I've got to go downstairs for dessert. They're waiting for me." Silence. "But I'm so glad you called. Really." *Oh, Colin, Colin, what's happening to me*?

"Sure," he said. His voice was hoarse. "I've got to go, too. I want to get a good night's sleep before tomorrow's session."

Amy's heart fluttered. There was a question she had to ask. She knew she had no right to ask it, shouldn't even be thinking it, but it came out anyway. "Are you having a good time with Brenda?"

"Terrific." Colin seemed relieved to be talking about her. "She was a hit at the workshop. Well, listen," he said, "I'll let you go."

Amy wanted him to say more. She wished *she* could.

Todd was standing just a few feet away from her now. She was talking to Colin. But she felt completely alone.

The receiver weighed a ton in her hand after Colin said good-bye. His voice resounded in her ear.

What she wanted more than anything was for Todd to vanish. Her shoulder muscles tightened. She shivered, not wanting to turn and face him.

She held the phone for what seemed like hours, torn between the voice on the phone and the boy in her room. She listened to the sounds of her breathing — short, fast breaths — and the drumming of her heart. Then Todd asked the question she dreaded hearing.

"Who was that?" His voice was curiously light.

Amy shook her head to help register those simple words. "A friend from Rose Hill," she answered. At once the pins in her dress seemed to jab her all over, numbing her. She flared her arms out a little. She felt fused to the tiny patch of carpet she was standing on.

Todd took two steps toward her. She sensed his nearness and turned, then smiled at him feebly. Involuntarily, her hand shot up to stop him.

He stared at her, red-faced, and helpless-looking. "I guess I should have left while you were talking," he said. "I'm sorry."

"Don't be." Her own words sounded shrill.

"I'm going downstairs," Todd said, obviously uncomfortable. "You want me to tell your aunt you'll be down soon?"

Amy nodded numbly. Todd's eyes searched her face as he passed her on the way to the door. "I'll see you a little later," he said. He touched her wrist. For an instant his fingers lingered there. Even when he'd gone her hand still burned. She closed her eyes and let out a heavy sigh. What was going on?

Chris Austin rested her chin in one hand and with the other tugged distractedly at her long blonde braid as she studied the clothes spread across her bed. "Which one do you think, Bren?" She looked anxiously at her stepsister to make sure she was paying attention.

"Hmm?" Brenda bolted upright from her curled position on Chris's other bed. "The blue," she said hoarsely, pointing to a royal blue silk

76

blouse. She was half-asleep. She and Chris had been consulting about clothes for almost an hour, and she was definitely losing interest.

Chris shook her head from side to side. "Sometimes I can't stand all this — all this time and effort put into trying to look right," she said. "If I were Laurie Bennington, maybe all this clothes stuff would thrill me. But I'm not. So I'm beginning to hate it."

"Why do you let yourself get sucked in then?" Brenda asked. "Wait. Let me guess." She paused for emphasis. "Politics. Dressing for success, right?"

"You'd better believe it," Chris acknowledged grimly. "And it starts right now. Working for Congressman Barnes last summer only gave me a taste of what my life's going to be like from now on."

"But you'll just be a freshman."

"I'll be more than that." Chris's voice was nononsense. "I'm running for office right away." She eyed the clothes disdainfully. "And to really get people to pay attention to my ideas I have to look right."

Brenda started to giggle. "But all these *suits*, Madame President."

Chris sputtered with laughter. She was used to people teasing her about her political ambitions. Everyone at Kennedy knew that she intended to be the country's first woman President.

"What about you, Bren?" Chris said, recovering. "Do you have any clothes you want to try out on me?"

77

"No," Brenda's voice grew quiet. "I don't think so."

Chris studied her intently. "Why are you looking at me like that?" She flicked her thick blonde braid behind her shoulder.

Brenda sat back. A noisy sigh escaped her. "I'm just going to miss you. That's all." Her eyes filled with tears.

Chris's eyes widened. "I'm going to miss you, too!" she exclaimed. She ran to Brenda and threw an arm around her.

"Oh, Chris," Brenda said, tears streaming down her cheeks now. "I guess . . . I feel like . . . I'm losing everyone," she confessed. "You, and — "

"Brad," Chris finished for her. She held Brenda away from her and tilted her stepsister's face up so she could look at her. "That's it, isn't it?"

Brenda shuddered suddenly, but she'd stopped crying. "Part of it."

"I don't understand. You were doing so well."

Brenda gently pulled away and stood up. "Chris, don't you see? This is my own house; my own family. I can't always be Miss Stiff Upper Lip. If I can't let my feelings out here, where can I?"

The shock on Chris's face quieted her. "Gosh, I'm sorry," Brenda said, slumping slightly. "I know you didn't mean anything, and you didn't deserve that blasting." A weak little smile crossed her face. She changed the subject. "Chris, have you seen Colin and Amy much lately?"

Chris looked puzzled.

Brenda shrugged. "Maybe it's all the counseling time I've put in at Garfield — " She hesitated. "But I think I'm picking up on something." She moved her shoulders up and down again. "Nothing terrible. Just that something may be a little off."

Chris was ready to ask more questions. "Listen," Brenda told her. "I've said too much already. I'm probably being crazy — "

"So what else is new?" Chris tugged at Brenda's hair. "I wouldn't worry about those two," she advised. "From what I hear, they're break-up proof."

"I'm glad," Brenda said honestly. "I don't know Amy very well, but she seems terrific. And as for Colin — " Brenda paused and rubbed her nose. "I think he could be a really good friend."

In her room later, Brenda closed her journal on the entry she'd been making. She propped her pillow behind her on the bed and leaned against it. A wave of sadness floated over her, and she didn't fight it.

A lot of times, she surrendered like that. She let herself think about Brad or about Chris leaving. Misery ran wild and her tears cleaned out her sorrow.

Expectantly, she pushed the play button on her Walkman, adjusted her headphones. "Swe-eet Love," Anita Baker wailed. Brenda felt the floodgates opening. She listened to her favorite song over and over again. Lying back, she clutched the small stuffed dog she'd named Garfield. Her tears came fast.

She was half asleep when the phone rang at eleven-thirty. Her eyes felt puffy and her skin was tight from crying. She ripped off her Walkman and leapt for the receiver, grabbing a tissue at the same time.

The receiver slipped out of her hand when she picked it up. She grappled with it and got it to her ear. "Hello?" she said. She wondered suddenly if something were wrong at Garfield. Then her face lit up with surprise. "Colin?" she said disbelievingly. "Colin, is that you?"

Chapter
10

"**B**renda, I — " Colin's hand still gripped the Austins' heavy door knocker.

"Sssh." Brenda opened the front door and slipped through the narrow space she'd left herself. The light from the hallway blazed behind her. It disappeared slowly as she backed into the night and closed the door.

"I'm sorry," Colin offered right away. "I know it's late. I hope I didn't get you into any trouble."

"You didn't. My dad is away on business. Otherwise — wooo!" Brenda said. Her heart went out to him, he looked so glum. She pointed to a narrow path that wound through a grove of trees beside her house. "There's a bench in the backyard," she said. "We can talk there."

Colin took her arm.

"I still don't understand," she said. He was pulling her along. "Why are you so upset?" She leaned back to stop him. He let go of her and turned. In the moon's soft glow, she could see how uncomfortable he was.

"Didn't you hear what I told you on the phone?"

"Of course I heard. There was a guy in Amy's room when you called her." Brenda shrugged. "So what does *that* mean?"

Beads of perspiration gathered on Colin's forehead. He looked imploringly at her, and she softened. "Okay," she said reluctantly, "*not* so what." He looked grateful. "But really, Colin, there are a million reasons why a guy could have been in Amy's room."

"Name two hundred thousand," Colin shot back with a straight face. He managed to grin when Brenda did.

"Maybe it was Andrea's fiancé who answered."

"It wasn't. I asked."

"Or her brother."

"No way. Andrea's an only child. Brenda," Colin said, "It was one of the ushers. Amy said so."

"You're no help!" Brenda looked Colin squarely in the eye. "So? It's a wedding. There are always loads of people milling around," she said evenly. "You can't know that something's going on."

"Of course I can't be sure," he snapped. He'd started walking again. Brenda took a few quick steps to catch up with him. "She just sounded weird. Guilty, or something," he whispered.

"Wait a second." They were in the backyard now, and the only sounds they could hear were the chirping of crickets and the occasional hoot of an owl. "Did the guy seem upset when he answered the phone?"

Colin thought a minute. "No," he said.

Brenda's eyebrows lifted slightly. "Nothing revealing like, 'Why do you want to speak with my girl friend?' "

Colin wiped away a smile. He rounded his lips into a perfect circle. "Nooo," he answered, drawing out the word. He shook his head in mock impatience. Brenda was laughing as Colin slid onto the bench beside her. At last, he seemed to be cheering up.

Brenda tucked her legs under her. "Here," she sputtered, "comes the really big question." She planted her finger on his chest. Colin looked at her quizzically.

"Was the guy out of breath when you picked up the phone? 'Cause if the guy was breathless then you're really in trouble — " She collapsed into laughter.

"Releasing a little tension, are we?" Colin asked. His tone was light but pained. He peered into the darkness. "I'm glad you think all of this is so funny. I bare my soul to you, and you make fun of me!" He had to fight back a smile. "It's a cruel world, Brenda," he said. "I can really see that now — "

Suddenly the light went out behind his smile. His shoulders sagged, and Brenda trembled.

"Look — " Colin's voice was strained. "I called you because there wasn't anyone else I wanted to talk to tonight, and I — I — " He looked straight into Brenda's eyes. "For the first time ever, I actually said out loud that I was afraid of losing Amy. I'd hardly ever let myself *think* that before." Colin slammed a fist into his thigh.

Brenda put her hand on Colin's arm. "I'm not making jokes, Colin. Really. But I understand why you think so, and I'm sorry." Colin acknowledged her words with a nod. He kept his eyes down. "I thought if I got you laughing, you — " Brenda hunched her shoulders and looked sheepish. "I guess I should have known better, huh? after all — " She straightened up and assumed a look of mock pride. "I'm a coun-sel-or!"

Colin didn't respond. He tilted his head back and gazed up at the starry sky. "It wasn't just that there was a guy in Amy's room," he said softly. "It's the way she spoke to me, the way we were with each other." He glanced over at Brenda. "She asked about you, by the way."

Brenda had a puzzled look on her face. "She did? What did she say?"

"Nothing much." Colin narrowed his eyes. "Why?"

Brenda shrugged.

Colin's forehead creased. He pressed the heels of his hands wearily over his eyes.

Brenda stared at her own hands and chipped away at the residue of nail polish on her thumbnail. Colin's mood had let feelings loose in her, the feelings she'd thought her crying jag earlier that evening had taken care of.

Tears stung just as fiercely as they had before. She knew she'd been teasing Colin as much to raise her own spirits as his. Now she didn't blink.

If she relaxed her eyelids for even one second, she'd be a goner.

The tears subsided finally, like a wave ebbing. She lifted her eyes to Colin's face. He was looking at her differently now — in a way that sent a blush rising upward from her neck to her cheeks and made her lower her eyes again. Was he trembling?

She watched him leaning toward her. She knew enough about how people behaved when they were lonely, and she knew what he was *really* thinking about. This was something she couldn't let happen. Softly she whispered his name. She put her hand to his chest, easing him away from her.

Colin meant no harm. She knew that. He just needed comfort — but only Amy could give that to him. But he didn't realize that, and Brenda smiled nervously, trying to think of something to say.

"Do you know what dumb things people try to do sometimes?" she came out with. "I've seen it at Garfield — when kids are having trouble with their relationships? They try to substitute someone for the person they're messed up about. Isn't that stupid?" She looked meaningfully into Colin's eyes.

Colin looked uncomfortable for a moment, then he smiled gratefully. His blue eyes gently mocking, he sank back into his seat.

"Yeah, crazy," he said.

Amy stared at the blueberry cheesecake on its elegant platter and cut herself a huge slice. The cake was so creamy it stuck to the cutter. She smeared the excess on the edge of her plate and glanced around the room.

She hadn't seen Todd since coming downstairs. Part of her wanted to ask her aunt or Phillip or someone — anyone — where he was. Another part of her used greater willpower than she'd used on the cheesecake. She headed from the dining room through the kitchen toward the back porch, vowing she'd stay out of sight.

Even though she wasn't with Todd, at that moment, she felt like a traitor. Loyalty. Faithfulness. They were such difficult words. Was she being faithful to Colin if she was being unfaithful in her head?

No one was in the kitchen. The lights were dim. The back door creaked when she opened it. She stepped out onto the large screened porch. As usual, the summer night air soothed her. Shadowy wild roses tumbled down the screen outside. It was very dark, except where the moon drew a path along the ground.

The wooden swing seemed to call to her from the other side of the porch. She walked over and sat in it, rocking it gently. So many memories surrounded her there in the Moores' backyard.

She felt safe, as if nothing bad could happen to her while she was curled up in the swing, hidden away by herself. She tucked her feet beneath the wide skirt of her silk dress. There she was, a little girl again playing little girl games.

But what was she supposed to do? Stay hidden forever? What would that solve? She had to see

Todd some time. She'd be walking down the aisle with him.

Amy cupped her chin in her hands and propped her elbows on her knees.

"Hello," a deep, honey-coated voice called softly. The kitchen screen door creaked as it opened. Amy squinted in the dark so she could see. "Can I join you?"

Amy gasped. Todd shushed her. He looked in mock horror over his shoulder. Stealthily, he tip-toed toward the swing.

"What's *with* you?" Amy swatted him playfully.

"They're after me," Todd said. He whipped his head to look behind him again. "You have to sa-a-ve me," he moaned like a wavering siren. He darted his eyes wildly and sank halfway to his knees.

"Will you stop it?" Amy said sternly. But she was laughing. She reached out and tilted Todd's head so she could look at him, then erupted into helpless laughter. He was snorting and making vampire sounds.

Amy rolled her eyes. "All right," she surrendered, playing along. "How am I supposed to save you?"

Todd stood up and pulled her to her feet. He set her dessert plate off to one side on the ground.

"What are you doing?" Amy asked. The excitement she felt made her shiver. She wasn't laughing anymore.

"What do you think I'm doing?" Todd asked huskily. Amy could hear him breathing. He leaned toward her, against her, whispering her name.

Amy backed into the swing until it pressed against her thighs. Todd came so close again she tumbled backward onto the swing, trying to escape his grasp.

He whispered suddenly into her hair. She could hardly hear him.

She placed her hands on either side of his face, but he wouldn't meet her gaze. She spread her thumbs across his cheeks and felt how smooth his skin was.

Todd looked straight at her now. "When I left your room I didn't think you'd ever want to see me again."

"But — "

"I mean it," Todd said fiercely. His eyes burned into hers. "And then I looked for you downstairs and I couldn't find you." He nuzzled her neck and she shivered. She didn't want him to stop, ever. "I thought you were avoiding me." Todd chuckled softly. "But I knew you were around," he whispered. "I followed your trail of cheesecake crumbs."

A smile bloomed on Amy's mouth, then faded as Todd sank down onto the swing beside her. He trailed his lips along her throat. She eased her head back slightly and his lips moved to cover hers. Compared to the warmth of his kiss, the summer air felt cool.

"I'm glad you found me," she breathed, moving closer to him. Her arms wound around his neck. She nestled her face into his shoulder. All thoughts of Colin, all thoughts of avoiding Todd, were gone. He pressed her even closer and she sighed happily. "We sure haven't done much talking," she said.

"Tomorrow," he promised. He looked at her, and she believed him. He kissed her again. She gave way and responded so completely this time, she was certain she'd remember this kiss all her life.

"Welcome back." Chris's tone was sharp, her arms crossed tightly across her chest. She glared at Brenda disapprovingly.

"What was Colin Edwards doing here?" She glanced at the clock in the kitchen, while Brenda poured herself a glass of milk. "It's almost one." Brenda looked at her. "If Dad had been home, Colin would have been hanging from the ceiling!"

"Well, Dad isn't home." Brenda spoke as calmly as she could. She hated it when Chris acted so hard, so critical. Her stepsister had become a lot less uptight in the past couple of years, but she still had her moments.

Brenda sighed. How could she tell Chris what Colin had confided to her? Especially with Chris looking so cross.

"Okay," Brenda said. Her voice was still steady. "I know the whole thing looks pretty odd. But will you please try to remember you're not my mother or teacher or somebody — and just be happy for me that Dad *wasn't* home? Come on," she said. She walked over and put her arm around Chris's shoulder. "I was just trying to help out a friend, okay?"

Chris rested one hand on her hip. Her lips

pursed as she bit at the inside of her cheek. "You're not going to tell me any more than that, are you?" she said. The hint of a smile touched her lips, but she kept her eyes narrowed as she studied her sister.

Brenda tossed her head from side to side and her silky brown hair swung with the movement.

"All right, all right!" Chris surrendered. "It's against all my political instincts, but I'm going to trust you on this and not do a number on you."

Brenda's eyes lit up. "Does that include keeping your mouth shut? I don't want *anyone* to know Colin was here tonight. He's got problems that no one needs to know about. It wouldn't be fair to him."

"Colin?" Chris said. She raised her eyebrow and winked. "Colin who?"

Chapter
11

Amy's eyes popped open at three in the morning. Grimly, she forced them shut. All she needed was for her mind to start racing again. Images of Todd had been creeping into her thoughts all night long.

She leaped out of bed. Susan stirred and made a contented sound. Amy looked at her enviously, stepping into her Chinese slippers and slipping her flowered cotton robe over her silky blue pajamas. Maybe a drink of water would clear her head and let her sleep.

The door to the bathroom was closed. Light seeped in under the door and Amy could hear water running. She stepped into the hall and waited.

The hall door opened finally. "Andrea!" Amy exclaimed. Her cousin's curly hair flew around her face. Her usual peaches-and-cream complexion matched the color of her red cotton nightshirt. "Are you okay?" Amy held Andrea away from her, checking for tears. "What are you doing in the guest bathroom?"

"Hey! Slow down, will you?!" Andrea beamed. "One question at a time. Yeah, I'm okay. I'm not crying." She thrust her face closer to Amy's for inspection. "And I'm using your bathroom because my sink's stopped up." Andrea looked down at her wiggling toes. A sheepish smile spread over her face. "I just couldn't sleep," she said, and her cheeks flamed even redder.

Amy raised her eyebrows. "I wonder why," she teased.

Andrea's eyes flared with mischief. She grabbed Amy's hand and dragged her into the bathroom.

"Are you crazy?" Amy squealed. She put her hand to her mouth to quiet herself.

Andrea stuck her head out the door and shot a look down each end of the hallway, then gently closed the door behind her. She wheeled around to face Amy. Her arms were crossed over her chest. "Crazy?" she said indignantly. "What do you mean — crazy? Are you so grown-up you've forgotten our famous bathroom talks?"

Amy smiled broadly. "Forgotten them? How could I have forgotten them? I *love* them!" Every summer, she and Andrea had shared at least one. It usually turned out that a middle-of-the-night conference saved one — or both — of them from going crazy. Over the years they must have spent hours talking about their deepest, most important problems.

Now a talk seemed terrifically appealing. Amy plopped down on the old needlepoint rug that covered most of the tile bathroom floor. Andrea snuggled in beside her. They used the tub as a backrest and tugged the rug in behind them for comfort.

Andrea reached for Amy's hand. She took note of their cramped quarters. "Not as roomy as my bathroom," she commented. Her face dissolved into a smile. "But it'll do."

Amy giggled. "You sure you want to do this? You may not look the part of the glowing bride tomorrow if you don't sleep enough."

"So! I don't care," Andrea declared. She squeezed Amy's hand tighter. "This is important. The next time we talk like this I'll be married." Andrea grinned. "Who knows what strange behavior I'll have picked up by then. Anyway — " Her face suddenly lost its brightness. "There's a chance Phillip and I will be moving out of state. We won't get to see each other so often."

Amy fixed her eyes on the underside of the porcelain sink and inhaled the scent of wisteria filtering in through the open bathroom window. "Relationships do change things, don't they?"

Andrea turned Amy's face toward her. "What was *that* supposed to mean?" She looked straight into Amy's eyes. "Let's have it. You don't have to put on an act with me."

"Will you stop being so understanding?" Amy pleaded. She didn't know whether to laugh or cry. In an instant, she was doing both. "This is ridiculous!" she announced, tears flowing down her cheeks. "I have nothing to be unhappy about!"

"Who are you trying to convince?" Andrea

asked softly. She reached behind her for the box of tissues on the shelf above the toilet.

Amy clamped her eyes shut. She shook her head furiously to try to stop the tears. But they kept coming.

It wasn't fair. She didn't want Andrea to see her like this. This was her cousin's special weekend. Suddenly she laughed out loud. "I guess I'm trying to convince myself," she said. She blotted her eyes with the back of one hand and took a tissue from Andrea.

"Oh, really!" Andrea said. Her hazel eyes danced.

Amy drew her knees against her chest and wrapped her arms around them. "The truth is, I don't know what's happening to me." She grinned. "Last year at this time I was sane."

Andrea nodded wisely. "Before love came along."

Amy nodded. "Exactly," she said. "Sane Before Love! Sounds like the name of a song." She hesitated. Only Andrea's welcoming smile made her want to keep talking. She poured out all her feelings about her parents' divorce, about Colin. Every once in a while, a shuddering sob took over. But once she started talking she couldn't stop herself. It was as if her words had a mind of their own. "And that isn't all," she said finally. She felt foolish. "I guess you noticed that Todd and I have been spending a little time together."

"A *little* time?" Andrea teased.

Amy just stared at her. "You think I'm terrible, don't you?" she asked. "Come on, tell me the truth."

Andrea got to her knees and put her hands on Amy's shoulders. "I do *not* think you're terrible," she said gently. "How could I think such a thing about my favorite cousin? You're a beautiful, wonderful person who just happens to be a little confused!" Andrea smoothed Amy's hair behind her ears and studied her face. "How can I help you?" she asked.

Amy pulled away. Her shoulders dropped. "You can't help me. I have to think things out for myself."

Andrea made a face. She rapped Amy on the head with her knuckles. "You *think* too much. That's your problem." After a moment of silence she said, "You know what?"

"What?" Amy asked glumly.

In a second, Andrea was on her feet. She pulled Amy up beside her. "It's definitely time for graham crackers and milk."

Amy smiled and stretched like a cat slowly. She and Andrea always ended up in the kitchen for graham crackers and milk after one of their talks. "*Definitely*," she said.

The kitchen was stocked for the wedding. There was scarcely anywhere to sit. Andrea made room at the kitchen corner between piles of platters the caterers would be using for the wedding reception. She set two paper cups and a carton of milk on the counter and dug in the cupboard for the graham crackers.

Amy felt content all of a sudden. Her problems didn't seem so bad when she talked things over. Settling into her stool by the counter, she poured milk into two cups.

95

"The problem is — " she began, "I may be in love with two people." She tore at the waxed paper covering the graham crackers. Eagerly, she dipped a corner of her cracker into her cup of cold milk. "Don't tell me not to think about *that*!" she said. She looked hard at Andrea.

Andrea smiled knowingly. "Todd *is* wonderful," she said simply.

Amy's heart nearly stopped. "Does he have a girl friend?" she blurted out.

Andrea took a graham cracker. Daintily, she nibbled at the edge. "I honestly don't know."

"Does Phillip know?"

Andrea wiped up a crumb of soggy cracker that had fallen onto the counter. She licked her finger. A wicked flame shone in her eyes. "I asked him about that the first time I saw you and Todd together."

Amy blushed fiercely. "And?"

Andrea shrugged. "Phillip didn't know. Todd stayed around school most of the summer. As a matter of fact — " Andrea looked as if she'd just realized something. "I haven't really had a chance to talk to him much since his spring vacation. Phillip hasn't, either." Andrea looked at her cousin sympathetically and leaned toward her. "So," she said gently, "I'm not much help, huh?"

Amy smiled weakly and tried to speak.

"What?" Andrea encouraged.

Amy gulped. "A lot of times . . . when I try to picture Colin's face . . . to remind myself how much I love him, how much he means to me — "

" — You see Todd's face instead," Andrea finished solemnly.

Amy shook her head up and down very fast. She didn't trust herself to say a word.

Andrea swiveled her knees from under the counter and placed her palms on her thighs. "What if," she said breezily, "I told you that was normal?" She stood up and slung her arm around Amy's shoulder. "Listen, little cousin, sure it's all confusing. Feelings never stay put in a safe little box. Life doesn't work that way — "

"Well, get you," Amy teased. She wiggled her index finger at Andrea. "The wise old lady here."

"No, really," Andrea said, and she was serious. "You'll go nuts trying to have everything make sense."

"But what do I *do*?" Amy demanded. All she wanted was some easy way out — a clean slate.

Suddenly she felt anxiety building inside her. Maybe she didn't even have to worry. Maybe Colin had fallen in love with someone, too — probably Brenda Austin. They'd spent almost an entire weekend together. If all this could happen to *her*, couldn't it happen to him, too?

She wiped the counter with a damp cloth while Andrea put away the crackers and milk. Amy tossed the empty paper cups into a trash can under the sink. For a few minutes, she managed to contain herself. Then halfway up the stairs, she poured out her confusions to Andrea.

"You know what I wish?" she said in a tight, small voice.

"What?" Andrea asked.

"If Colin *is* having a fling — and boy, I'd deserve that — I hope he isn't hurting as much as I am now." Amy buried her face in her hands and cried. Andrea held her. "See how crazy I am?" Amy said, looking up at last. They sat together on the landing. "Last night, when I was with Todd, I wasn't even thinking about Colin."

"You're not crazy," Andrea comforted. She stroked Amy's arm. "And you're not terrible, either. You wouldn't care this much about how Colin was feeling if you were." She tilted Amy's tearstained face up to look at her. "Can you believe that?"

Amy nodded slowly. The sigh she let out came from the deepest part of her.

Andrea shook her head. "And as for what you should do now — who can tell you that? No one. Believe me, I know." She put her hand on Amy's shoulder. "I've made plenty of mistakes in the three years I've got on you." She shrugged quickly. "So you'll probably make some, too."

Amy looked sideways at Andrea. Her eyes narrowed with curiosity. "You've made more mistakes than you've told me about?"

Andrea's grin stretched from ear to ear. "A lot more," she said. She slipped her arm around Amy's waist and, side by side, they climbed to the top of the narrow stairs.

"Promise me," she said, clasping Amy's forearm, "that whatever you decide tonight, you'll try to enjoy yourself. I want you to enjoy my wedding. If you're miserable, all you'll have left are bad memories." She looked straight into Amy's eyes, and the weight of the world seemed to rise off Amy's shoulders.

Amy had no idea what she was going to do about Colin or Todd. But at that moment, she couldn't have cared less. She threw her arms around Andrea so hard she almost pitched them both down the stairs.

Then suddenly she felt very selfish. She'd been so busy worrying about herself, she hadn't let Andrea get a word in edgewise. She was probably crazy with nerves about the big step she was about to take.

"Don't worry about it," Andrea comforted when Amy apologized. "You owe me one. That's all." Her eyes were teasing. "You think I'm going to run out of problems just because I'm getting married!?"

Chapter
12

Amy scrambled out of bed and sprang toward the bathroom at a sprint. Susan stepped out of the way to keep from getting bowled over.

"Why didn't you wake me up?" Amy accused. "The wedding's at two. Were you going to let me sleep until it was *over*?"

"It's not that late," Susan said. "Just ten o'clock." But she looked genuinely ashamed. "We were all having breakfast and talking. I was helping Aunt May get ready for the caterers. Jim got here about a half an hour ago," she reported. "He's been following me every second."

Amy nodded as she began to brush her teeth. "Uh," she grunted, angling her head and pointing at Susan's silk-screened yellow T-shirt. "When did you get that? I like it."

"Thanks," Susan said, glancing at her watch. "Listen, I'm going downstairs. Jim says he wants to talk to me. We're meeting under the elm tree in the front yard. This is my big chance to tell him to get off my back."

Amy cupped water into her hands and rinsed her mouth. She heard Plume barking. "You'd better wear lip guards," she teased, wiping the toothpaste from the sink. She splashed warm water on her face and patted her cheeks with a fluffy blue towel.

"Amy!" It was Todd's voice.

"You didn't tell me Todd was here," Amy said. Blood rushed to her cheeks.

Susan shrugged apologetically. "I thought he'd be gone by now. He and Jim came over to help Uncle Sid set up tables before the caterers get here. Todd said he'd be going right home and asked me not to wake you. He only lives a few miles away."

Amy headed for the hall window that overlooked the backyard. She stopped in her tracks, seeing Susan glare at her. "What are *you* looking at?" she asked good-naturedly.

"You!" Susan started to smile. "All that guy has to do is say your name and you get the goofiest expression on your face."

Amy scowled slightly, then laughed, picturing how she must have looked. She clutched her bathrobe to her and hurried the rest of the way to the window. The lace curtains blocked her view. She swished them to one side, then struggled with the sash, lifting it higher.

"Todd?" She looked out over the sun room to where he was standing under the massive oak tree. The screen made him look fuzzy. She slid it up. "What's the matter?" she called. Even from

101

so far away, she could see the worry on his face.

"I need your help," he shouted up to her. "Quickly. Will you come down?" He was peering at something by his feet.

Amy's heart leaped into her throat. Susan was behind her then, looking over her shoulder.

The rest of the family was standing off to one side near the huge green-and-white striped tent that would be used for the reception. Plume was yipping now. Andrea patted his head and talked to him, but the small black dog strained at his leash.

"I'll be right there," Amy said, her voice quavering. She slammed the screen shut and rushed back into the bedroom, yanking off her robe and pajamas.

"Here," Susan said. She pitched Amy a faded pullover and jeans. Amy slipped them on in a matter of seconds. She smoothed her hair and stepped into her sneakers. In one minute flat, she and Susan were downstairs. They flew through the sun room's double doors to get outside. Jim was just ahead of them.

Amy skidded to a stop near the trunk of the oak tree. Todd was stooped over a furry little animal. Amy couldn't see what it was — only that it was hurt. In the split second it took her to walk gingerly over to them, her experience with Sam flashed through her mind.

"What can I do?" she asked. Then, looking down, she breathed in sharply. A baby rabbit lay at Todd's feet.

"It's okay, little guy," he murmured. He kept

trying to see where the animal was injured. "This pretty lady and I will take care of you."

Amy felt herself go limp. Todd glanced up at her then and smiled. Amy thought she'd never seen a face so handsome. No matter what happened between them, she knew she could never forget the way his eyes melted into hers, the way she felt so much a part of him. She knew she'd never want to forget.

She squatted beside him to inspect the bunny. "So — " she said. She tried to control her quivering chin. "What should we do?"

"Well, we shouldn't really touch him, but we can try to clean the wounds and keep him warm," Todd said evenly. "Get me a bowl of warm water, and some clean cotton." He thought a minute. " — And something I can use as a bandage."

Amy stood up. She could see the rabbit's heart was beating fast — too fast. "Do you think he's in shock?"

All Todd's attention was focused on the little bunny. His teeth clenched. "Maybe," he said. "Must have gotten jumped by a neighbor's dog. Plume's been on a leash all morning. Let's just try to stop the bleeding. After that, we'll take him to Dr. Victor's."

Andrea motioned to Amy. "Stay there. I'll get the stuff you need." She thrust Plume's leash into Jim Dunne's hand.

Uncle Sid stepped over after the bandaging was done. He peered into the box Todd had put the brown rabbit in. The older man glanced at his watch. "It's already after eleven," he said. He seemed reluctant to say anything more.

Aunt May joined him. She linked arms. "They have to take the animal to the vet *now*, Sid," she told him. "They can't wait till later." Her voice was quiet but firm.

He nodded. "It's not that I don't care about the little thing — " he said.

"Don't worry," Todd said. "We'll be back in plenty of time for the wedding, I promise."

Queen Anne's lace lined the road they were driving along. Behind it stretched the stubble of harvested cornfields.

Amy sighed happily. She and Todd had finally had a chance to talk, to get to know each other. She shifted slightly in her seat. She held the rabbit's box securely on her lap. The animal lay motionless except for the rise and fall of his breathing. Amy felt helpless watching him. She'd always loved animals, but the feeling had really grown stronger lately. It had begun to seem to her that all living things were connected somehow.

"Do you even like spiders?" Todd asked, grinning.

"I do," she declared. Todd looked surprised and pleased.

"Ever see the webs that golden-orbed spiders make?" he asked.

Amy nodded enthusiastically. "Once I counted fifteen in one tree." Amy could hardly believe how comfortable she felt with Todd. It really seemed like fate had brought them together, that they'd spent their whole lives up until now getting ready for these few brief days. But she was frightened, too. It seemed impossible that in just one day they'd be drifting back to their separate worlds.

For a few minutes, they sat in silence. The weather couldn't have been more perfect for a wedding. For as long as she could, Amy wanted to hold on to the feeling soaring inside her.

"It's so beautiful here," she breathed.

"Very beautiful," Todd echoed. Out of the corner of her eye, Amy saw him looking at her, his face radiating a warm glow. His arm slid around her shoulder. He tugged her to him. She regarded him with an astonished look.

"Doctor!" she exclaimed. She slid closer to him, keeping the small brown carton from bouncing as she moved. "Our patient!"

Todd pretended to be puzzled. "But that's why I wanted you near me! Didn't you hear the little guy calling my name?" Amy snuggled into the crook of Todd's arm. "Where are we?" She straightened up slowly and looked around. Now, every once in a while, cottages dotted the view.

"About twenty-five miles west of your uncle's. We're almost at the vet's. See that dirt road up there? That's it."

A few minutes later Todd turned the car into a bumpy, potholed driveway. "Hold on tight."

The driveway wasn't long. At the end of it sat a rustic-looking clapboard farmhouse. Todd waved at the slim, stately woman who'd come out to greet them.

At first, Amy felt out of place. This woman —
and Todd — knew so much more about animals
than she did. Inside her clinic, Dr. Victor's hands
worked swiftly as she disinfected the rabbit's
wound and rebandaged it.

"You two did a fine job," she said. She let her
eyes rest on them for just a minute. "Are you
going to be a vet, too?" she asked Amy.

Amy blushed. "Well, I've thought about it."

"Good," Dr. Victor said bluntly. She peered
down again at her patient. "The world needs
more women vets."

Todd smirked. "Do I detect a touch of female
chauvinism?"

"Not at all, Mr. Stanton," the doctor said in a
friendly voice. "Not every man — nor every
woman, either — has your sensitivity." She took
off her red-framed glasses for a moment and
rubbed her eyes. "Now you two better get going.
Call me tomorrow morning and I'll tell you how
our patient's doing."

"Dr. Victor really likes you," Amy said to
Todd on their way to the car.

Todd grinned in a way that made him look
like a hopeful, wide-eyed little boy.

Suddenly Amy noticed what time it was. Her
knees nearly buckled. She held up her wrist for
Todd to take a look.

"Uh-oh," she grunted. "A quarter to one." His
ruddy face paled slightly. His hand dug into his
pocket for his keys. "It's a good thing I called
Phillip before I left and asked him to bring my
clothes — just in case I didn't have time to run
home and change."

Amy giggled.

"What's so funny?"

"Oh, nothing. I was just thinking how lucky you are to have Phillip. He always seems to be bringing you your clothes."

Todd snorted good-naturedly. In the car, while he was driving, Amy let herself imagine what it would be like to share her life with him. She imagined a farmhouse in the country somewhere, like Dr. Victor's, where the two of them would open their private practice. She gave in to the urge to hug him.

"Hey!" he said, braking. The car swerved slightly and Amy eased away. "I'm driving!"

"Sorry," she said.

"What was that hug for, anyway?" he asked innocently, glancing with pleasure at Amy's flushed cheeks and gleaming eyes.

She felt silly and gave a little shrug. Todd drew her closer and she settled in beside him. "I don't know," she began. Then she giggled. "I guess I heard you calling my name."

Chapter
13

Amy streaked up the stairs and nearly crashed into Susan, who was coming through the guest room doorway. Amy's mouth fell open. "You look *gorgeous*!" she said, eyeing her perfectly made-up, taffeta-clad sister enviously.

Susan gave a dry little laugh and held her nose. "*You* don't!"

"Whew! I know." Amy grimaced good-naturedly. Using Susan as a steadying post, she stood inside the doorway. She yanked off her sneakers and pitched them into the room beside the rocking chair. "Did Mom get here yet?" she asked.

"Uh-huh. About two minutes after you and Todd drove out. She called last night. I didn't have a chance to tell you this morning, with all the commotion."

"How's Sam doing?"

"Fine." Susan threw her head back and laughed.

"What's so funny?"

"You. You have as many animals in your life as you have boyfriends."

Amy wagged her finger at Susan. "Your turn'll come," she predicted. "One day you'll be somewhere and whammo! — some guy with a magic smile will look at you and you'll fall like a ton of bricks."

Susan's eyes and mouth widened in mock disbelief. "Me?" she said. "Never." But Amy was already heading for the bathroom.

"I'll be in Andrea's room," Susan called after her as the bathroom door closed. She held out her nails to examine them. "I want to spend some time with her before she's a married lady."

Amy couldn't believe it. The wedding was actually going to start on time. Even the maid of honor, who had just flown in from Seattle that morning, had arrived on time. Now she stood huddled with Amy, Susan, Andrea, and Aunt May in the dining room. Amy had stolen a few minutes to be with her mother, who was now seated in the sun room. The sliding door was shut so no one could peek in. But guests could be heard greeting one another.

Aunt May linked arms with Andrea. "Sounds like a full house out there. You sure you want to go through with this?"

"Yessss!" Andrea answered, laughing. Her head went up and down at a furious speed and her veil flapped. She looked like she'd been waiting the whole weekend for someone to ask her that question. Amy had never seen her so deliriously happy. Andrea's laughter was so contagious, everyone joined in.

"That sure, huh?" Susan teased. Again the dining room rocked with laughter.

The door rumbled on its track and Uncle Sid's face appeared. He squeezed half his body through the opening he'd made.

"May! What are you doing in here?!" His voice overflowed with loving impatience. "The music's going to start any minute!"

Amy pictured the guests seated, waiting, the minister poised to begin, Phillip standing by his stepfather, palms sweating. She took a tight little breath. A shiver traveled up her spine. Todd would be waiting, too.

"Just look at our girl," Uncle Sid said as Aunt May walked over to him. He was all the way in the room now, his eyes fixed on Andrea, his hands clasped behind his back. He shook his head slowly, as if Andrea were hypnotizing him by being so beautiful.

"Daddy!" she protested. She gave a short embarrassed laugh and turned so he couldn't see her.

"Daddy, *what*?!" He dashed to kiss her.

Andrea closed her eyes. She shook her head disbelievingly. "Just . . . just . . . *Daddy*." She released a resigned sigh.

"Uncle Sid?" Amy said gently. His face was so red, she was worried about him.

"What, you beautiful girl? You all look so

beautiful," he said. "You know that?" He swept his arm to include her and Susan and Andrea and Rochelle, the maid of honor.

Amy swallowed a smile. She raised her eyebrows, indicating Aunt May, who stood by the door. An amused expression played on her aunt's face. Uncle Sid went an even deeper shade of red.

"And this — " he said. He lunged and threw his arms passionately around Aunt May, " — is still the most beautiful woman of all."

"Aww," the girls chorused. They exchanged fluttering glances.

"Sid! Stop it!" Aunt May said. She shooed his arm off her shoulder. But she was smiling.

Suddenly her expression changed. She slid the door open farther and made a shushing motion. "This is it!" she said. She gave an excited little toss of her head when she looked back at everyone. Her eyes were dancing till they rested on Andrea. Then they misted. Andrea ran to her mother.

Soon the group was moving fast, smothering squeals. They traveled through the main hallway — past the rainbow-colored wrappings of gifts heaped high on the mahogany library table, through the fragrant scents of aftershave and perfume the guests had trailed behind, until finally they reached the closed curtained doors of the sun room.

Amy heard the piano music. She started trembling as Aunt May opened the door slightly to make her entrance. Anxiously she wondered if her legs would support her when her time came.

111

Through the crack where the door hinged, she saw her mother sitting on the aisle in the second row. Dee had arrived just before the wedding. She was across the room, stooping and stretching to get pictures.

As soon as Aunt May was in her seat, Uncle Sid went and stood beside Andrea. Every so often Andrea nervously fingered the seed pearls that were sewn onto her ivory-colored dress in a delicate pattern.

Watching her cousin, Amy felt a surge of pride. She blushed and smiled when Andrea caught her staring.

"How can you stay so calm?" Amy whispered.

Andrea smiled slyly. "Who's calm?" she whispered back.

Amy beamed at her. She adjusted the puffy pink sleeves of her bridesmaid's dress and tried to force away her own nervousness. When Susan grabbed her hand and squeezed it, the butterflies in her stomach fluttered again.

Then Phillip's stepfather and mother walked down the aisle. Phillip's mother took her seat. His stepfather took his place beside Phillip. Jim appeared from where he'd been standing just inside the sun room's wide doors along the back wall. Susan smiled politely at him. Jim's smile surged beyond politeness. Susan inhaled sharply and took his arm. Her eyes looked everywhere but at his face.

Amy peeked to look at the guests. They were angling toward the aisle, entranced. Uncle Sid had slid his hands into his pockets. His eyes wandered restlessly to the ceiling. He whistled a faint, tuneless melody.

Amy sighed. Almost desperately, she huddled closer to Rochelle and Andrea. Now it was her turn. She saw Todd's eyes on her from his position across from where Jim had been stationed. He stood at the head of the aisle, his eyes sending her the message that she looked beautiful. Now it was her eyes sweeping over him, the sight of him thrilling her. She began walking, slowly, rhythmically. But her mind was racing. Tomorrow this magic would be over. Todd would slip back into his life. She would be back in Rose Hill.

She felt her eyes brimming with tears as he watched her long march down the aisle. His gaze flooded her with tenderness. Her lips tingled with the memory of his kisses. She knew then what she knew the first minute she saw him — that if he wanted her — reached for her — she could never resist him.

Chapter
14

It wasn't long before the reception was in full swing. Amy could scarcely reach her cousin to congratulate her, but Phillip wasn't having any problems getting close to his new bride. His arm hadn't left her waist since the ceremony ended.

Pink-lined tablecloths covered tables on the lawn between the sun room and the tent, where food was being served. A four-piece combo was tucked off to one side.

Amy smiled. She'd been watching her uncle whirl her aunt around the patio. Looking at them made her feel like singing. At that moment, they were proof that love could last.

Giddy, suddenly, she yearned to do away with her own tangled feelings. Well, at least she wasn't falling to pieces. Somewhere in that lay a small victory. She took a deep, determined breath. She would not, she resolved, allow dark thoughts to ruin her day.

Her stomach rumbled so she strode into the tent. A selection of hot entrees sizzled alongside salads and an ice sculpture shaped like a swan that miraculously hadn't melted in the oppressive August heat. Tucked around the ice were jumbo shrimp and crab legs.

Todd was off in a corner of the tent talking to Phillip. They stood beside one of two huge fans. Amy was about to wander over to them, when someone tapped her on the shoulder. She whirled around in surprise, just as a flash went off. "De-ee!" she complained.

"Geez," the young photographer said, ignoring Amy's protest. "Couldn't your family have ordered cooler weather for this wedding? Or put ten more fans in here? The temperature goes up five degrees every time I take a picture." She grinned. Then her eyes narrowed slightly. She looked straight at Amy. "So . . ." she said. She popped a shrimp into her mouth after dipping it in cocktail sauce, then chewed it thoughtfully. Swallowing, she cocked her head in Todd's direction, then stared coolly at Amy. "You two seem to have become good friends. Are you ever going to introduce us?"

"Sure, I'll introduce you," Amy said abruptly. "If you promise to stop looking at me like I'm the Wicked Witch of the West. I have so much to tell you, Dee," she said, " — so much I don't understand. Please. Go easy on me." She looked quizzically at Dee. "You're still my friend, aren't you?"

Dee's cool expression was softening, but her face was serious. "Of course I'm your friend," she said. "But I'm Colin's friend, too, Amy." She glanced down and played with her camera strap. When she raised her eyes, they were filled with concern. "I just wish you'd try to see how this all looks from an outsider's viewpoint."

Amy piled some Swedish meatballs on her plate and waited.

Dee sighed deeply. "I came up here to take pictures, right?" Amy just stared. "I arrived with love and kisses for you from Colin: my friend; your boyfriend. But you were so busy mooning over this other guy — a guy I don't know, a guy Colin certainly doesn't know — that you didn't even ask — " Dee said in a low, husky voice that didn't sound like her own, " — how Colin *is*." She leaned forward. A pained expression settled on her face. "What am I supposed to think, Amy?"

"I don't know," Amy said honestly. She put down her plate. The afternoon sun was shining through the open tent flap. She squinted, then angled away from the brightness.

Dee sighed. "Listen," she began. She blotted the perspiration on her forehead with a napkin. "I don't even know this — what's his name?"

"Todd."

"I don't even know this Todd."

"Not *this* Todd! *Todd*."

Dee flipped up a hand in apology. "Okay," she said. "Todd. Anyway," she went on. "If you . . . like him," she said haltingly, "he must be all right." She managed a smile.

The corners of Amy's mouth turned up faintly. Her stomach flipped. She looked at Dee. "Do you

116

hate me?" she said. Dee looked confused.

"No, I don't hate you," Dee said. She slung her arm around her friend. "Tomorrow we'll have more of a chance to talk. And I really will try to understand what's been going on here."

"I know," Amy said. "All I ask is that you don't make any judgments." She flashed Dee a pleading look. "At least, not yet. Will you promise me that?"

Dee hesitated a moment, and Amy's breath caught. Then her friend smiled her slow, familiar smile, and Amy felt Dee squeezing her shoulder. "I guess I could manage that," Dee said.

"Great." Amy mustered a begrudging smile as she noticed Todd heading straight for them, so handsome in his usher's formal suit. His posture looked confident and sure, like a movie star's. She didn't care if she was staring. Dee's eyes were on him, too. He quickened his pace.

"Hello!" Todd said warmly when Amy introduced them.

"Hello, yourself," Dee came back. She'd been priming her camera.

Todd shifted shyly but kept smiling. "It feels a little weird meeting one of Amy's friends from Rose Hill," he said. "I don't know much about her life there." He held out his hand. "Anyway, you look like a good person to start with. It's nice to meet you."

Dee swung her camera to one side and shook his hand. "Nice to meet you, too," she answered, a touch too awkwardly, Amy thought. She panicked for an instant, then smiled with relief when Dee issued Todd her usual open smile.

"Get a load of that!" she said suddenly. She glanced beyond him. "Two sets of in-laws enjoying each other's company? That's a real rarity these days." She exchanged her 50mm lens for a 200mm telephoto.

Amy felt Todd nudge her. His eyes said he wanted to be alone with her. Amy slid her hand into his. "We'll talk to you later, Dee." She hesitated. "Okay?"

"Okay," Dee answered distractedly. Her mouth and chin were the only parts of her showing behind the camera. She dropped low and steadied her lens.

A moment later Amy was locked in Todd's arms behind a tall hedge bordering the lawn, and Dee was the farthest thing from her mind.

Todd drew back to look at her. He stroked her hair off her forehead with his gentle hands. "I want" — he brushed his lips over hers as he spoke — "to take you" — he kissed her once more — "away from here."

Amy tingled all over. She couldn't resist his kisses. But she forced herself to pull away, out of his embrace. Slowly, she dropped her arms to her sides. How could she *leave*?

"It wouldn't be right to leave," she said. The muscles were hardening in her neck. "Everyone would be angry. I'd be mad at myself, too, especially if we left before Andrea cut her wedding cake and threw her bouquet."

Inside, her heart was actually sinking. She knew her words weren't firm enough — Amy had left the door open for them to go somewhere together later. And she knew it would be wrong.

"No problem," Todd said. He checked his watch and kissed her upturned nose. "It's just four o'clock. I can wait. A little while, anyway. But let's take five more minutes, Amy. I'm not ready to rejoin the crowd yet."

"Okay." Amy gave in and led Todd over to a bench on the lawn. As they talked, she wished she could stretch the minutes they were stealing into hours.

Todd leaned back, his long muscular legs stretched out in front of him. Amy sank back against his chest. A blackbird called from a nearby branch. They both turned their heads to look at it.

Todd smiled slowly. "Have you noticed how much in-tune we are?" he asked.

Amy smiled back at him. It was true. Even now, as they focused on the bird, it was as if he'd been reading her mind.

He shrugged. "It's hard to tell for sure," he said. "After all, we haven't exactly known each other for years." He scratched his head thoughtfully. "But, you know, when we were at Dr. Victor's, and I was watching you watch her work. . . ."

Amy snuggled closer, feeling dreamy. "What?" she murmured. She loved the way his voice sounded, smooth but slightly gravelly, as if he'd just awakened from a long sleep.

He looked at her intently. His words spilled out. "When I was looking at you, I knew I'd never felt this way before," he said.

After tomorrow, she might not see Todd again. The thought tore at her heart, but made her feel

119

braver, too. Amy rested one arm on his chest and ran her finger back and forth along his lips. She could feel his heart beat beneath her arm.

Her breath almost stopped when he turned his head to look at her. She stayed still while his eyes explored her face. He turned slightly, so they were eye to eye, then reached for her. His lips gently grazed her forehead, her eyelids, the tip of her nose. She thought she'd faint with pleasure before he ever reached her mouth. But at last his lips settled over hers and melted into her.

"We have to go," she whispered when they broke apart. She could hear her uncle making an annoucement from the tent.

"I know," Todd sighed. He kissed her again, then laughed when neither of them made a move to leave.

"That *means*," she said in a sultry voice, "you have to let go of me."

"You first," Todd teased. He covered her face again with quick, staccato kisses. "If you wait for me to let you go, a million years from now they'll find us fossilized right on this spot."

She removed her arms from around him and he stood up. Then he reached down for her and pulled her to her feet.

As they entered the tent, Uncle Sid was announcing Andrea's and Phillip's first official dance as husband and wife.

Amy listened closely to the words of the song. It was a bittersweet melody. In a way, the words fit her feelings about Todd. They told the story of two people who found each other unexpectedly and fell in love, people who saw each other only once in a while and knew each time they were together there was a chance they'd never meet again.

Amy didn't realize for a moment, but listening to the song, watching Phillip lead Andrea across the floor, she'd been holding her breath.

"You now what?" Todd whispered, sweeping Amy into his arms as they began to dance, "I almost kissed you while we were walking up the aisle?"

Amy laughed. "That would have been adorable."

Todd held her away from him and he smiled. Then his eyes darkened suddenly. He stopped dancing. His arms stayed around her, and he stared at her, his face completely serious.

"Oh, Amy," he sighed, his voice flooded with emotion. She buried her face in his neck and felt him swallow. The way he'd said her name had scared her and she felt a strange fear spreading over her, slowly, the way ink spreads on paper. She couldn't stop it. And even worse, when she took Todd's face in her hands and made him look at her, when she explored his eyes, she couldn't see herself there.

Phillip's BMW was parked in front of the house. He leaned back against the hood. "Hey, Andrea!" he called up to the second floor balcony. "C'mon, gorgeous! The place won't wait!"

"Here. Here. Here." Uncle Sid was passing out rice. He pressed a spoonful into each guest's hand.

"Don't you think this is a little corny?" Susan whispered. Amy shrugged.

"On the contrary," Todd said. His eyes gleamed mischievously. "I think it's a little ricey." Susan and Amy groaned.

At last Andrea came rushing out of the house onto the front sidewalk. She clutched her bouquet of roses and baby's breath.

"Throw it! Throw the rice!" Dee squealed, pitching her handful.

Amy felt stoked with energy. Her dark moment with Todd was like a bad dream now. She threw as hard as she could. Her rice and everyone else's showered down over the newlyweds' hair and clothes.

Andrea swirled to face the guests, and Amy held her breath as her cousin prepared to toss the bouquet.

Andrea turned away again and sent the bouquet flying over her shoulder. Amy could almost feel the ribbons tangling in her fingers. She knew it was headed straight for her. She gave a little cry as it landed in her arms.

She buried her face in the flowers, turning the bouquet from side to side so she could feel the petals on her cheeks. Then she froze. An image of Colin's face flashed before her, then quickly dissolved into one of Todd. She closed her eyes. She didn't want to see.

Chapter
15

"You're *where*?" Dee said. It was seven-thirty. She'd been packing up her cameras to go home and had picked up the Moores' phone when it rang. Most of the guests were gone and the family members were in the backyard. "*At a coffee-house!*"

"Right," Amy said. "The reception's mostly broken up, right?" She knew she sounded defensive. She shifted restlessly in front of the coffeehouse pay phone and shook her head. It was crazy to be here. Everyone was staring at Todd and her, still in their wedding outfits. But she was having the time of her life.

It was hard to calm down, probably because what she heard in Dee's voice matched what she was already thinking. "Hey, listen," she said. She tried to keep her voice steady. "Remember what you promised. Let's wait till I get home before you tear into me."

"Fair enough," Dee said. She laughed. Then she hesitated uncomfortably. "In the meantime, Amy, what should I tell Colin if I see him?"

"You don't have to tell him anything," Amy said. She took a breath. "So," she began, changing the subject, "Are you going to the workshop tomorrow?"

"I hadn't thought about it," Dee said. "I'll see how I feel about it when I talk to Marc."

"Dee?" Amy said hesitantly. She felt like she was about to dive into an icy pool.

"What?"

"Do you think — well, do you think Colin has his eyes on anyone?" Amy glanced over at Todd. He'd ordered dessert. Now he was waving to tell her they'd been served.

Dee thought back to when she last saw Colin — at the workshop the night before. "Well, I know he likes Brenda," she answered. Then suddenly she realized what Amy was getting at. "But just as a friend, I guess."

"You *guess*?!" Amy said. Dee's answer threw Amy so off balance that she had to quickly say goodbye. Amy hung up the phone and walked slowly back to the table. As soon as she sat down, Todd reached across the table for her hand. Why did Dee's answer make her panic? Now she couldn't look at Todd. In front of her was the dessert he'd ordered for her as a surprise. Chocolate mousse pie. Her face contorted as she stared at it.

"Rather have cheesecake?" Todd grinned at her. Amy pasted on a smile and rubbed her finger along the edge of the plate.

Someone or some*thing* was getting back at her — chocolate mousse pie was Colin's favorite. It wasn't Todd's fault she felt like this.

She let his eyes rest on him for a moment. He was still looking at her. He hadn't eaten much of his Napoleon, but she slid her own dessert over to him. Humoring her, he took a bite. It was a sure thing that in a second he'd say something that would shake her out of the funk she was in and send her soaring again. She just wished he'd hurry up!

Driving home to Rose Hill, Dee felt herself frowning. She rubbed her forehead. Amy wanted her to hold off any judgments until they talked, but seeing Amy and Todd together all afternoon had really upset her.

It was easy for Amy to ask that Colin not be told anything. But Dee worried about that. If she ran into Colin, the truth — whatever that was — would probably be splashed all over her face.

Now, as her car reached the Rose Hill town limits, she realized what a difficult position she was in. She felt like a slice of baloney sandwiched between two pieces of bread.

No one was home when she got there. She shut the front door behind her and set her equipment down. Her cat, Lily, leaped off a nearby chair and dived to rub her legs. Dee smiled. She scooped up the snow-white cat and nuzzled her neck. Lily meowed loudly.

"Hungry, are you?" Dee asked fondly. Lily released an even louder meow in response. Dee served up a can of Salmon Supreme into Lily's dish, then headed straight for her darkroom to calm down.

It wasn't long before she was lifting the black-and-white glossies dripping from the chemical trays. She studied the wedding pictures closely, groaning when she saw one she'd taken of the couples on the dance floor. It wasn't that the photo wasn't good; it was *too* good. Todd and Amy were in it. They looked like they were the lovestruck bride and groom.

Dee knew she was going to burst if she didn't talk to Marc. Yes, she'd promised Amy she wouldn't tell Colin anything until they talked. But she hadn't said she wouldn't tell Marc. He would probably be home from the workshop by nine-thirty. Just time enough for her to soak in a musky-scented, lukewarm tub and consider what to say to him.

She knew from the moment she stepped from the tub that she would tell him. The urge didn't seem so awful — sharing this kind of secret with the boy she loved. Talking with Marc wouldn't hurt Colin or Amy.

In five minutes, she was dried and dressed. She untwisted the wide straps of her cotton jumpsuit, then smoothed her hands over her hips.

At nine-thirty, Marc's voice told her everything she wanted to know: He missed her. He loved her.

"You should have been at the session today!" He sounded like he'd been to a pep rally, not to a tutoring seminar.

Dee reached down to buckle her sandal. "Was it as good as the one last night?"

"Better."

Dee hesitated. "How are Colin . . . and Brenda?"

"They're fine," Marc said innocently. "I think they're having fun together in the workshop."

"Oh?"

"What do you mean 'Oh?' "

Dee could almost see Marc frowning. "Oh . . . nothing." She thought a minute. "Marc? Can you meet me at the sub shop in twenty minutes?"

"You took the words right out of my mouth."

"Good," Dee said solidly.

"That 'good' sounds pretty heavy. What have I done now?"

"Don't get all hung up," Dee teased. "I'm just a little inside out, that's all."

"You mean, as of today?"

"I guess so."

"What went *on* at that wedding?" Marc asked. His voice wavered. "You still love me, don't you?"

"More than ever."

"Well, that's a relief. I thought you'd met a dashing young photographer up there, and you guys were leaving on the midnight plane for Kenya."

"Not this year," Dee teased. She ran her fingers through her short hair.

"Not *any* year," Marc insisted. "Hey" — His voice turned low and inviting — "Let's hang up. I can't wait to see you."

Most of the seats at the sub shop were taken when Dee arrived. She found Marc back in a corner and wove her way between the picnic tables toward him. Eagerly, she dumped her handful of glossy prints a safe distance from Marc's tuna sub, then sat down beside him.

"Come here, you," Marc ordered lovingly, swinging one leg so he was sitting sideways on the bench. He leaned back against the wall and pulled Dee toward him into a hug.

Marc swung his leg back over the bench and faced the table. "Want a bite" he offered. He held up his sub for her to taste.

"Of you," she teased. She took a fake mouthful of his upper arm.

"Watch it!" He elbowed her off. "There are laws against wounding star soccer players."

"Only if you bite their feet," Dee smirked.

Marc wiped his mouth and hands with a napkin he took from the dispenser on the table. He eyed the photographs. "Are these from the wedding?" He began working his way through the glossies. He nodded approvingly and winked at Dee. "Pretty good, there, lady."

He whistled softly when he came to the picture of Todd and Amy on the dance floor. "Geez," he said, "Who's this guy?"

Dee's eyes narrowed. She shook her head. "Doesn't look good, does it?" She bit her lower lip. "But I sure don't want to think what I'm thinking."

"Which is," Marc coaxed. He slurped down the last of the orange soda he'd been drinking and eased Dee closer to him.

Her shoulders sagged miserably. "I'm afraid Amy and this new guy — who unfortunately seems to be terrific — are really crazy about each other."

128

Marc crushed his empty paper cup. "What about Colin? Did you ask Amy about him?"

Dee's spirits sank even deeper. "Yeah," she said dully. "I asked her. But she was so involved with the wedding and with this guy, she hardly had time to answer me. The main thing she told me was that she had a lot to talk to me about when she comes home tomorrow — and that naturally, I shouldn't say anything to Colin."

"Pretty nice," Marc said sarcastically. He rested his forearms on the picnic table and hunched over them. He shook his head and looked disapproving.

Dee read his face and suddenly felt herself shift to Amy's defense. "Now wait just a second, mister," she said to Marc meaningfully. "I remember a time when people could have made some serious judgments about *us*. Do you remember those times, Marc?" she asked lightly.

Marc reddened. He stroked his chin thoughtfully. "Hmmmm," he teased, "give me a minute." Dee laughed and kissed the tip of his nose. "Maybe Amy's planning a surprise party for Colin," he couldn't resist saying, referring to the series of misunderstandings he and Dee had somehow managed to survive, and then the birthday party Dee had planned for Marc.

"Well, then," Dee said, as if she'd decided something for him. She played with the sun-lightened hair on Marc's arm. "Hands off?"

"Hands off," Marc said grudgingly. Then she added, "But not off me, okay?"

"Definitely not," Dee said.

"Well, for *that* privilege," Marc said, "you have to listen up. It's *my* turn to talk."

"About what?"

"What do you mean, about what? The *work-shop*!"

Dee missed the impatient look Marc shot her. The owner of the sub shop was beckoning so energetically in her direction, he looked as if he were waving a plane into its landing position. Next he put one fist to his mouth, another fist to his ear, and made the sign for phone call.

Dee raised her eyebrows and pointed a fore-finger at her chest. "Me?" she mouthed. Sam nodded vigorously.

Dee dashed back in a minute to tell Marc that Fiona had tracked her down. "Her car's not run-ning," Dee explained, "and she needs a ride to a ballet dress rehearsal. It's tomorrow and she has to get up really early in the morning, so she's stay-ing at another dancer's house. Anyway, she prom-ised the girl she'd be there tonight."

"You want me to go with you?"

Dee thought a minute. "No," she said. "It'll be late when I get back. It's forty-five minutes from here. You need your beauty sleep for the session tomorrow."

"Aren't you coming? I thought you wanted to take more pictures."

Dee shook her head. "No, I don't think so. I want to save my energy for my talk with Amy." She made a face. "Somehow I think I'm going to need it. Hey," she said then, "don't look so dis-appointed." She grinned at Marc. "Will you call me tomorrow some time after the workshop so we can carve out a few hours to be together?"

Marc brightened immediately. "What time?"

"Six?" Dee asked. She started backing toward the door.

"Perfect. If I'm not home, I'll call you from Colin's. We may be having an after-the-workshop evaluation meeting." He reached across the table and pulled her back to him for a good-bye kiss.

" 'Bye," she whispered. She let her eyes linger on his face for an instant, then reluctantly made a dash for the door. Marc stared after her. She was gone by the time he noticed she'd left her photographs behind.

He stacked them neatly and chewed off a hunk of sub. Glancing up, he saw that Brenda and Colin had come in. They'd taken a table near the register.

Marc scowled. He wasn't just surprised seeing them there. He was downright uncomfortable. He'd seen them spend a lot of time together at the workshop. That seemed fine — business and all that. But now they were laughing together, and Brenda was ruffling Colin's hair. This didn't look like business.

Chapter
16

By nine o'clock, the moon was full and high. The road curved and dipped like a neverending ribbon ahead of Todd's car. Fresh summer air floated through the open windows.

Todd drove slowly. A deer had made an ill-timed leap across the road, startling him — and Amy, too. Amy didn't mind the reduced speed. What she really wanted was for the trip from the coffeehouse to her Aunt May's to last forever.

A wistful feeling washed over her. She wiped a windblown strand of hair from her eyes, then leaned against Todd's shoulder. His hand slid up her arm and cupped itself around her cheek.

Amy swallowed painfully, pressing back tears. Every gesture of love now was bittersweet. The magic weekend was growing rapidly — too rapidly — to a close.

She tilted her head to look at Todd. She didn't know what would happen after tomorrow, but tonight she wanted to memorize Todd's face, to sear its image into her memory.

She snuggled near him again. She couldn't get close enough.

"I have a surprise for you," he said.

"You do! Where?" She turned and made him lean forward so she could slide her hand between his back and the seat. He squirmed when she tickled him. "Come on, tell me," she said. She even reached under the blanket that covered the rips in the upholstery.

Todd laughed. "No, no, no," he teased. He said each word lower on the scale. "Not that kind of surprise." He drove past the turn-off for the Moore's.

"Well, *what* then?" Amy waited for Todd to speak.

"This." Todd looked mysterious. He made a left hand turn onto a dark lane edged by woods on both sides. The road narrowed, and grew bumpy, making Dr. Victor's driveway seem as modern as a freshly blacktopped highway.

"Where are we going?" Amy protested lightly.

"Hey," Todd admonished, "be patient."

Amy didn't have to be patient long. The road climbed for a hundred feet, opened into a hilly clearing. The hills surrounded a lake, spotlighted by the moon. The meadow glowed.

"I know it's hard to see at night," Todd apologized, "but I think this is the prettiest spot around. Every time I come home from school I visit this place." He reached for Amy and brushed her face with kisses. "Tonight," he said huskily, "I wanted to share it with you."

133

He turned off the ignition, and in place of the idling engine they could hear familiar country sounds. The headlights turned the fields and trees into a ghostly paradise.

"Wait here," Todd said, looking mischievous. "I'll be right back." The car door opened with a creak and he leaned over to give her one last kiss. "Keep watching," he said.

"I will," Amy promised, as if she could really take her eyes off him. As if she'd ever want to.

He began picking wildflowers. They seemed to be growing magically in the streams of brightness the headlights made. His hands filled with them. He thrust his arms up and did a swooping dance, then blew extravagant kisses at the car.

Amy laughed. She tried to resist the prickly feeling that had invaded her body.

Colin's strong face sprang up in front of her. Now it gave way to Todd's. Had she really come to love him? Her fingers rose to cover her mouth, as if saying the words would make them real. After talking to Dee, she'd confess her unfaithfulness to Todd and Colin. She owed them the truth. She wasn't being fair to either one or them, or to herself.

What she longed for was one clear moment, one tiny capsule of time to untangle the confusion, to find the way to do what she knew was right. Certainly, this wasn't the moment. It wasn't even the *day*! She felt more like silly putty then flesh and blood.

A siren blasted a piercing, undulating wail from a nearby town. Todd stretched his neck skyward and matched the sound. He sent his voice howling up and down like a wolf's.

Amy laughed out loud and clapped her hands. She made the sound, too, and Todd rushed back to the car. He turned off the headlights. In an instant, the flowers were nestled on the back seat. He tore around to her door and opened it for her. His eyes lured her out of the car. He took her hand and led her into the meadow.

The moon was enough to see by. It spread the lake with light. Amy could make out the hills that rose on the lake's far side.

"The flowers," she whispered, tilting her head toward the car. "They're beautiful."

He turned. "Not half as beautiful as you," he said, and he wrapped her in his arms. His skin felt hot where it touched her. When he kissed her, he tasted like chocolate mousse pie. He framed her face with his broad hands.

The love she felt burned in her throat, gathered behind her eyes collecting tears. Why did everything about this glorious night have to be so perfect?

A breeze swept down from the hills then. It swirled around their feet, then up, up, as if it could whirl them away together, forever.

"It's a hot night," he said suddenly.

"It is," she said. She, too, became aware of the mugginess again.

"Come here." He led her to the edge of the lake where water lapped and gurgled through a narrow stretch of stones and sand.

"Amy," he said, gazing down on her. His voice

was choked with feeling. He stretched his arms toward her. She lifted her hands. He gripped her wrists and pulled her up to him, spreading his hands across her back and pressing her to him. "I've never felt like this," he whispered hoarsely. "I. . . ."

Amy knew then he wanted to tell her that he loved her. But she didn't want him to. He'd already shown her that in a hundred other ways, and she was afraid she'd fall apart if he really said the words.

Her lips slid up his smooth neck to his chin and found his lips. He gently slipped his arms around her back and stroked her bare shoulders.

"Promise me — " Todd began. He tenderly but firmly drew her head back and lost himself in her eyes. A curl fell onto his forehead. Amy swept it back. "Promise me you'll remember tonight, that you'll remember me."

Amy thought she was going to explode like a cork released from a bottle of champagne. Giving a small cry, she held onto him fiercely. "I'll remember. I will!" she told him. His breath was hot on her ear. He whirled her around and around until she laughed and cried all at once, squeezing the magic from every minute — every second — they had left.

"Will you look at this?" Brenda stared down in disgust at the catsup sinking into her hot pink oversized shirt.

Colin gave a sympathic nod. Then he grinned. He pointed to her collar. "The next stain would look perfect right there," he teased. Brenda laughed and reached over to ruffle his hair.

They'd been filling themselves with fries at the sub shop. Colin had spotted Marc in the corner. He'd waved just as Brenda bit into her fry and soaked herself with catsup.

"I'm going to get some water for this," she announced, standing up. For a second, her forefinger rested lightly on her slightly pursed lips. She looked pleasantly puzzled.

"The thing I don't remember," she said, "is whether I'm supposed to use cold water or warm water, or whether I'm supposed to run the stain or blot it, or let it soak in or let it dry up, or — "

"Enough!" Colin said. He covered his head with his arms.

Brenda's eyes sparkled mischievously. "You wouldn't happen to have a copy of *Hints from Heloise*, would you?"

"What rotten luck," Colin said, deadpan. "I gave away my last copy two days ago."

"Sure you did," Brenda said cheerfully. She headed for the counter. On the way, she patted the wooden Indian that stood guard over the sub shop.

Colin smiled. Because of Brenda, he'd almost recovered from his disappointing phone call to Amy.

Now she was consulting with the ever-smiling sub shop owner about her stain.

Marc got up from the table, Dee's photographs tucked snugly under his arm. Bread crumbs fell from his lap to the floor. He reached for the check, lingering over the numbers longer than necessary while he contemplated how to handle his exit. Of course he had to stop and say hello, but what would he say?

He'd promised Dee he wouldn't interfere with Colin and Amy's relationship. But what was going on — *might* be going on — between Brenda and Colin, that was a different matter, wasn't it? Couldn't he say something to Colin about that?

Brenda was at the counter. As Marc walked by her, he put his hand on her shoulder, briefly. They exchanged hellos. He walked up front and paid his bill at the register, then he headed over to Colin's table.

"Hey, old Workshop Wizard," he began.

Colin grinned. The glossies under Marc's arm intrigued him, and he reached for them. "Did Dee take these?" he asked.

Marc grabbed for the photographs before Colin could get a hold of them, and they all tumbled to the floor. The incredibly romantic one of Amy and the guy from the wedding lay on top of the pile staring up at them. Colin bent to pick it up.

"Hey!" Marc yanked it out of his hand. "Personal property, buddy."

"Oh, come on!" Colin said. He snatched the print back.

Almost instantly, his grin dissolved into a dark scowl. He trained his eyes on Marc's stricken face, searching for any explanation that would be less painful than the one that seemed obvious. "Who is this guy?" Colin asked, his voice strained.

"And what's he doing with *my* girl friend?!" Marc shrugged helplessly. He gathered up the photos, slipping the one of Todd and Amy from between Colin's fingers.

Just then Brenda came back. "Find it," she said to Colin with a grin, stretching her shirt out for him to locate the spot.

He stared blankly at her. At once, she sat down beside him and put her hand on his shoulder. "Colin?" she said. "What's wrong?" She looked up at Marc's grim face.

"I've gotta go," Marc said uneasily. He reached over Brenda and gave Colin a light punch to his upper arm. "You take it easy, man," he said. "Okay?"

Colin moved his head numbly, and Marc walked away. But before Brenda could say a word to Colin, Marc walked back. His eyes swam with pain. "Colin," he said.

Colin didn't look up. "What?"

Marc jammed the car keys he was holding into his pocket. He gripped Colin's shoulder so hard, his knuckles turned white. "I'm sorry," he said. "I am really sorry."

He left with the photographs clasped tightly under his arm. Brenda crossed over to her own bench. She entwined her fingers in front of her and leaned toward Colin. "Want to tell me about it?" she asked.

He didn't meet her eyes.

She tried to stay relaxed by reaching for a fry and shoving it around in some catsup. "Colin, if you want to leave now, I'll understand. . . ."

Colin's face turned the color of a blank sheet

of paper. "I guess I don't want to stay too long," he told her. He rubbed his neck and managed a weak smile. "You should be glad to hear that. I'm not exactly charming company right now."

Brenda waved him off. "You sure you don't want to talk?"

Colin shook his head and shifted uneasily. "Not yet," he said. "*You* talk."

Brenda's eyes glinted. "Okay, but you'll be sorry."

Colin looked puzzled.

"Once I get started, you won't be able to shut me up."

"I'll take my chances," he said.

Brenda grew serious. For a moment, she closed her eyes. "I know what it's like not to want to talk about your feelings," she said. "When Brad and I split up, there were days that putting two words together felt like a major effort."

Colin nodded sympathically.

Brenda stared at her hands. The sub shop had never seemed so empty and quiet.

"I still feel like that sometimes," she explained. She smiled but her eyes were sad. "There I am, breezing along like I'm terrific — *cured* — and whammo! Something reminds me of Brad, and I feel as if I'm sliding to the bottom of a deep, dark canyon."

Colin looked at her intently. "But you climb again, right? And each time the canyon doesn't seem as deep."

Brenda brightened. "That's it! That's exactly it!" Then she hugged herself suddenly. Her eyes filled with tears. "Colin," she murmured, "I still miss him so much!"

Colin felt his own eyes burning. He hurt for Brenda. He hurt for himself, picturing what his life would be like without Amy.

"Here," he said. He handed Brenda a huge stack of napkins. She laughed nervously. "Sliding again?" It was more a statement than a question.

Brenda grinned through her tears. She nodded and Colin looked warmly at her. "I'll catch you before you hit bottom," he said.

Chapter
17

"It's kind of late, isn't it?" Mrs. Atkinson surveyed the bedraggled pair standing in front of her brother's doorway. She leaned out and stared at the star-studded sky. "Did I miss a hurricane or something?" A small smile crossed her face.

Amy glanced at Todd. She felt the glow of their time together beginning to fade. "I'm sorry if we worried you," she said. "What time is it anyway?"

"Ten-thirty."

Todd breathed out a heavy sigh. "I'm sorry, too, Mrs. Atkinson. It's my fault we're so late."

Amy put her hand on Todd's arm. Todd and her mother had spoken briefly during the reception. Amy knew that the talk had been hard for her mother; she liked Colin so much. Now she was trying not to look disapproving.

"No way," Amy said, trying to smooth things over. "Don't listen to him." She looked confused.

"Didn't Dee tell you where I was?" She slid off her wet shoes.

Her mother shrugged. "Dee said something about a coffeehouse. But it could have been in Greece for all I knew. Besides, I got a call from you-know-who while you were gone.'

"Your office," Amy groaned. "Don't tell me." She held her hand across her eyes like a fortune-teller in a trance. "They're having a meeting at two in the morning and they want you to be there.'

Her mother wore a pained expression. "You're close," she said. "The meeting's at nine."

"On Sunday morning."

"Anyway," Mrs. Atkinson said, waving her and Todd inside, "I'm all set to drive back. Susan's upstairs packing."

"Go back? Tonight?" Amy almost screeched the words. For the first time, she noticed her mother's overnight bag on the floor by the library table. She glanced helplessly at Todd. "Do you have to go to the meeting? Can't we leave tomorrow the way we planned to?" The words stuck in her throat. "Oh, please, Mother!"

"I'll drive Amy back tomorrow," Todd broke in.

Mrs. Atkinson looked from one to the other. "Well, I — "

"Oh, *please*," Amy begged. There was so much more she had to tell Todd. In the midst of her agony, her heart went out to her mother. Why shouldn't her mother look so confused? Less than two days ago, her eldest daughter had been madly in love with Colin Edwards — *only* Colin

Edwards. Now she was pleading for more time with a boy she'd just met.

"All right," her mother said. Amy sagged with relief. "Todd can bring you home — but under one condition." Mrs. Atkinson's lips curled into a wry smile. She wagged her finger as she spoke. "You have to promise; no more midnight coffee shop trips."

Amy and Todd both laughed. Amy wanted to run and put her arms around her mother, or at the very least to have a good talk. They hadn't done that for a long time.

Mrs. Atkinson started down the dimly lit hall, toward the kitchen. "I'm going to have some tea while I'm waiting for Susan," she said. She paused and called over her shoulder. "You want some?"

"I'd love some, Mom," Amy said. Every minute spent with Todd was precious to her, but she didn't want her mother to be alone now.

Todd read her eyes. "No thanks, Mrs. Atkinson." He waved.

"I'll walk you out," Amy said.

When the front door closed behind them, Todd took her hand. He led her to the car and kissed her slowly, before climbing into the car.

"I thought *my* life was a soap opera," Mrs. Atkinson said to her daughter. She eased honey off the spiral wooden stick and watched it sink into her red zinger tea.

Amy was in her bathrobe now, just ready for a long talk with her mother. She reached for the ceramic honey pot. She couldn't believe that

144

she'd actually told her mother all the questions whirling in her brain. Did Todd really love her? Could a girl love two boys at once? What would happen tomorrow? Would Colin talk to her? Or would he go off with someone new?

"Tune in tomorrow," Amy said with a grim smile. She studied her mother's concerned face. "How did you get through it?" she asked.

"The divorce?"

"Mmmmm."

Betsy Atkinson held up three fingers and counted off each one. "You. Susan. Work. That's how I got through."

"Do you still miss Daddy?" Amy asked.

Her mother looked melancholy. "Sometimes," she said. Then she smiled. "But the right thing happened."

Amy leaned closer. "Did you ever think you wouldn't make it?"

"Only about a hundred times a day."

"Really?"

Her mother puffed with mock pride. "Now I'm down to thirty times a day," she said.

Amy sat back and digested that. The silence was broken only by the hum of the refrigerator. "Until the wedding — " Amy said. She hesitated. "Susan and I — we thought you were so — so together again," she finished lamely.

Her mother threw up her hands. Her eyes went wide. "Surprise! Don't you know half the people walking around with grins on their faces are really hurting inside?" She sat back and looked at her daughter. "You're like that," she pointed out. "I've seen you. And it's hard, isn't it?" She patted Amy's hand. "Trying to hide your feelings."

Amy nodded. "I wish I could let them out more," she murmured. "Especially where Colin is concerned." Just saying his name, Amy felt a rush of warm feeling.

"I'm going to call him," she announced abruptly. She stood up.

"Now?" Her mother looked at the kitchen clock. "It's almost midnight!"

Amy suddenly felt light-headed. "I don't care, Mom."

"But what are you going to say to him? You haven't got your feelings straight."

Amy heaved her shoulders up and down and grinned sheepishly. "I may never have them straight." She planted a kiss on her mother's forehead. "I'll see you tomorrow," she said.

"What about Todd?"

A thoughtful expression flickered on Amy's face. "That's a whole different matter." She disappeared up the stairs. Then she poked her head back into the kitchen. "Mom?"

"What, dear?"

"Thanks."

"Who are you calling?" Susan asked. "Are you coming home with Mom and me?" She'd come out of the guest room and was juggling suitcases to take downstairs.

Amy pointed to the mouthpiece of the hall phone. Now the phone in the guest room wasn't working at all. "Colin," she mouthed silently to

Susan. Then she whispered. "And Todd's driving me home tomorrow."

Susan looked as if she'd keel over. "Colin?" she bleated. "Todd's driving you home, and you're calling *Colin?!*"

"Sssh," Amy said. She pointed to their aunt and uncle's bedroom.

Susan still seemed in shock. Her blonde pony-tail swung back and forth. "I don't understand you," she said. She started tiptoeing down the stairs, then glanced back. "I think we need to talk!"

Amy giggled, then went quiet as she returned her attention to the phone. Someone had picked up in Rose Hill. "Rich?"

"Yeah?" The young athlete sounded sleepy.

"It's Amy."

"Oh, hi, Amy. How — "

"Hi," Amy interrupted. "Is Colin there? I know I'm calling pretty late — "

"No problem." Rich paused. "I don't know why Colin didn't pick up. Maybe he's in the bathroom or something." Rich yawned loudly. "I'll check."

Amy tried to unknot a clump of her tangled hair. The wait seemed forever. And the next sleepy voice on the phone was still Rich's.

"Geez, Amy, I don't know *where* Colin is. He called at about ten — after the workshop let out — and said he was meeting someone at the sub shop. I don't know who, though."

Amy felt like she was falling from a cliff. She drew in the inside of her lip and gnawed at it.

"That's all right," Amy told him. What could she have said to Colin, anyway? That she thought she still loved him but had something to tell him that would break his heart?

"What a minute. It was Brenda," Rich said. "Brenda Austin. That's who Colin said he was meeting." He hesitated. "That's funny — " His voice echoed Amy's silent shock. "I thought he'd be home by now. How's Susan?"

"Oh fine. She's on her way back to Rose Hill right now." Amy couldn't possibly talk any longer so she mumbled a good-bye and slowly let the receiver sink to its cradle.

In her mind's eyes, she saw Colin in front of her. He was smiling, straight into her heart. Amy pressed her palms to her eyes. Her tears slipped out between her fingers. In less than thirty-six hours, she — and no one else — quite possibly could have destroyed her own happiness. The worry about Colin she'd felt in Rose Hill? It seemed like heaven compared to what she was feeling now.

Her uncle's house wasn't a castle anymore. She wasn't a princess — that was for sure. The hall clock struck twelve. The magic was over.

Chapter
18

"Amy, are you all right? I've been looking for you."

Amy peeked around the trunk of the old oak. She'd propped herself against it just after dawn, and was thinking. Her aunt walked toward her from the house. "I'm fine, Aunt May," Amy said. "Really." She stifled a yawn. Again and again, she'd been going over in her head what she should say to Todd about Colin. More than anything, she didn't want to hurt him. It would break her heart if he thought she'd been leading him on all weekend.

Aunt May's eyes twinkled. She removed her cordless phone from the roomy pocket of her apron. "Todd wants to talk to you," she said. " 'Dr. Victor's victorious' he said to tell you — or something odd like that."

"The rabbit!" Amy nearly fell over herself, grabbing the phone from her aunt's hands.

Aunt May laughed and let go. "You don't need to *tackle* me!"

Amy blushed and mouthed an apology. Her aunt winked. She headed back across the wide green lawn.

"Todd?" Amy's great resolve crumbled when she pronounced his name. She leaned her elbow on the wrought-iron table near the tree and gripped the phone. "Is it true? The bunny's going to be all right?"

"It's true." There was a smile in Todd's voice. "He's even eating. Dr. Victor said he'll be fine."

"Can we put him back here? I mean, can you — ?" Amy felt her excitement draining away. This was *their rabbit* she and Todd were talking about, and suddenly she wanted to see it. But what good would that do? *Todd* would be taking care of the rabbit. Not her. Amy shivered slightly. Today was the day she had to let Todd go.

"We . . . I can try," Todd stammered.

There was silence then. Amy took a quick breath. "Can you still drive me home?" she asked.

"Sure."

"When?"

"Is twenty minutes too soon?"

Amy's heart leaped. She cleared her throat. "No," she said, trying to keep from flying straight up into the air. "It's fine."

She laughed to herself when she got off the phone. Tears of relief glistened on her cheeks. It was Sunday, the day she and Todd would say good-bye. The moonlight was long gone, but still Todd wanted to be with her. During the course of her long, sleepless night, Amy had talked herself into believing he didn't really love her. She wiped the tears away with the big cotton shirt she had on over her Levi's and retied the knot of her blue scarf.

On her way to the house, a craziness fizzed inside her. She grappled with it, trying to force it away, to feel about Todd the way she knew she should. Her time with him was just fantasy — a romantic weekend in the country that she had to say good-bye to. That's what she'd been telling herself. But she didn't want to say good-bye, not yet. How could she expect that of herself? She'd only just said hello.

The old Chevy rocked as if it were crossing railroad tracks. "I am only dreaming this," Todd said. "I do not have a flat tire."

Amy's heart went out to him. Since he picked her up, he'd seemed so edgy, uptight, not at all the way he'd sounded on the phone. They'd pulled out from the Moores' driveway about ten minutes earlier and now were on the two-lane road that would take them all the way to Rose Hill.

Todd exhaled a noisy whoosh of air. He eased the car onto the shoulder of the road.

Amy hardly knew what to say. But it was one of those times when she felt she had to say *something*. "It's a good thing I've only got one bag," she kidded, "in case I have to walk."

Todd half-smiled, but scooped her toward him. His lips grazed a kiss on top of her head.

She drew back from him, as she would have from a stranger. A boy could put his arms around you or kiss you and still seem light years away.

She was sure Todd cared about her. It was understandable that he'd be upset today. She knew he didn't want her to go. But something else was going on. She could feel it.

He slapped his thighs lightly, as if trying to jar himself into action. "I'd better get to it," he said. "This tire isn't going to fix itself."

"I'll help," Amy offered. She didn't wait for a response. She opened the door and ran around the car to the trunk. Todd got out, too. He took a minute to get a closer look at where they'd gotten themselves stuck. Then he threw his head back and laughed out loud.

"Are you out of your mind?" Amy asked. She followed his eyes to find out what he was laughing at. The road seemed to stretch forever. All she saw were wildflowers and scrub and what looked like the entrance to a driveway. Todd seemed to be enjoying a private joke. Amy scowled slightly. What was so funny about a flat tire in the middle of nowhere?

He slipped his arm around her waist and brought her gently to him. "See that?" he asked. He leaned his head close to hers and pointed to the driveway. An amused grin spread across his face.

"I see it," Amy said, but she still didn't know what was so funny.

"How quickly we forget," Todd teased. He held her closer and his face grew serious. "That innocent-looking driveway," he said, "is the road we took to paradise last night."

Amy's legs went rubbery. Suddenly, she wanted to stand with Todd again by that lake, in that meadow. She didn't know why for sure. Maybe being with him there in broad daylight would make her come to her senses and see that their time together was really ending. Only then could she tell him about Colin.

She locked her suitcase in the trunk and dragged him toward the driveway.

"What about the tire?" he reminded her.

"We'll fix it later," she told him. For a change, she was the one creating the surprise. *She* was the spontaneous one. But Todd wagged his head at her as if she were out of her mind. Then he stopped resisting her. Sighing noisily, he crooked his arm loosely around her neck. As they walked the half mile to the clearing, Amy's insides fluttered.

Daylight hadn't destroyed the setting. The meadow was lovely. The lake shimmered. A circling breeze made the wild flowers dance.

The deeper she and Todd walked into the meadow, the more Amy knew she had to start thinking — *fast*. If she couldn't get everything out quickly, she'd be lost.

But the speech she planned to give about Colin had vanished from her mind, as if someone had broken in and stolen it. She tried to piece together new sentences. But Todd was touching her again. The words were tumbling together in her mind and making no sense.

"I wish I had *four* flat tires," Todd whispered. "Then we could be together longer." Slowly his hands smoothed her arms and swept across her sun-warmed back. Without meaning to, she slipped closer to him.

"Todd," she murmured. She said his name again and again. Insistently, his fingers combed through her hair. Fanning the long silky strands around her head, he kissed her — so deeply she thought she'd drown.

Then she thought of Colin and stiffened. At once, Todd backed away. He searched her face, his eyes glazed from their kisses. A light had gone out in them.

"Why did you do that?" he said coldly. Amy felt like she'd been struck. "Why do I feel you growing so distant?" He let his hands drop from her shoulders. Amy watched his foot toy with a stone, and her neck hardened into knots. She tried to control her voice. But even before she spoke, she felt it rising above her normal range.

"You do it, too!" she said. "Yesterday while we were dancing. Today, in the car!" She could hardly get the words out, but some part of her was relieved that the fantasy was shattering.

She stood frozen, expecting Todd to deny what she'd just said. Instead he went limp. He shrugged. "Maybe I *am* distant . . . sometimes," he told her.

His words stung. She could have asked him to explain, but she stopped herself. If she did that, she'd be stalling again. Worse. She'd be hanging what she was telling Todd on what he was telling her. For once, she wanted to speak from a point of strength. She sensed, somehow, that it would make her feel less lost.

A horrible silence rose between them like a wall. Amy turned. She walked toward a large, flat rock that edged the lake. As she moved the hot wind billowed her shirt behind her. She looked back and motioned for Todd to follow her.

"*Please*," she urged, when he just stood staring at her.

He gave the stone at his foot one swift kick, then caught up with her. She sat down. Todd's face was a mask of pain. Squatting next to the rock, he shielded his eyes from the sun and studied her face.

She bent toward him. "Todd, listen to me. This is so hard, but I have to tell you something." Her voice shook slightly, but the risk felt true and good. She knew that it was right to tell him.

"Go ahead," Todd said tightly.

"The call Friday night," she began, "while you were in my room?"

Todd nodded and looked confused. Amy reached up to touch his face. He flinched, and her hand dropped to her lap.

"That guy isn't just a friend, is he?" Todd asked.

Amy couldn't look at him. She tugged stubbornly at a weed that rose between a crack in the rock. Her lip trembled.

"Honestly — " she said. She focused on Todd now, and her own eyes were swimming. "I don't know *what* Colin is to me anymore." She took in a short, sharp breath. "I haven't spoken with him since then. Maybe he hates me. Maybe he's off with someone else by now." She knew she didn't have to go on but she couldn't stop herself. "Maybe the word's out in Rose Hill that I went away for two days — just two days — and fell in love with someone I'd never seen before."

Todd touched her hand. She felt his eyes swallow her. "Fell in love?" he asked quietly. "Are you sure?"

She shook off his hand. "Yes!" she cried. Then she moved her head back and forth very fast as if she were trying to clear it. "At least, I think so! Oh, Todd, how am I supposed to know what I'm feeling?" Her shoulders sagged. She hid her face in her hands. Her hair cascaded over her fingers. "I don't even know where I am anymore."

Todd brushed her hair back. "With me," he said gently. He peered at her to see if she was going to be all right.

"That's what *you* say!" Amy sputtered through her tears. She threw her arms around his neck. "Todd, this is all so nuts!"

"Yes. We're two together people who just happen to be losing it."

Amy ran her hand along his cheek and moved close to him. She stared at her feet and realized she felt calmer since her outburst.

She reached for Todd's hand. "Why isn't anything simple?" she asked him. Her eyes held his. "Why couldn't I have come up here and had an uncomplicated weekend, then run back to my boyfriend, guiltless and pure?"

Todd laughed.

"Or why couldn't I have come up here with no boyfriend at all?" Amy said. A groan of longing escaped her. "Oh, Todd, I loved you. I did — I *do*. But maybe I still love Colin, too. Is that possible?" Her breath caught. "Please, *please*," she said, "tell me I'm not horrible." She sniffled into her arm.

156

"Oh, Amy, you're not horrible," Todd whispered. "Don't think that." He smoothed her face and hands with tender strokes she couldn't bear. Not really wanting to, she stood up. Todd must have sensed what she was feeling. In a moment, she felt his arm gently encircle her waist.

"I don't want you to blame yourself," he said. "Do you think I'm *dumb*? I knew that guy — Colin — was someone special. If he wasn't, you wouldn't have looked as if the world had collapsed when he called. But I kept after you anyway. Even after I saw how confused you were. If that wasn't *horrible*, I don't know what is!" He slammed his fist into his thigh. His shoulders gave way. He sat down again on the rock and put his head in his hands. Then he looked up at her, plaintively. "I'm sorry," he rasped. "I knew there would be pain like this." Shaking his head, he rose and reached for her again, pulling her into his arms. "There were moments I was glad you pulled away," he said. "When you did that, I swore to myself I'd leave you in peace, but just one look at you and — "

Amy pressed Todd's hands between hers. She spoke in a small, strained voice. "Do you think it was the moonlight and the wedding that got to us — that we were in love with all that and not with each other?" She let out a small sob. "Todd," she faltered, " — what if we never have a chance to find out, what if we never really know what we were feeling?"

"I don't know what happened up here," Todd said. "But, Amy — " he groaned, "whatever it was, I'm still feeling it. Right now, that's all I

157

know." Todd's eyes were so sad, Amy's heart ached for him. "I just wish — " He broke off suddenly.

"*What* do you wish?" she asked anxiously.

He put his finger to her lips to hush her. Almost desperately, he kissed her till her mouth tingled. Trembling, she relaxed against him. All thoughts banished. She sensed these last few hours together might have to last them a lifetime.

"Todd!" she said. "What is it?!" He'd gone limp in her arms. A fast pulse throbbed at his temple. He didn't turn away, but he didn't look at her, either.

"I'm not being fair to you," he said. His voice was trembling.

Amy stared at him defiantly. "What do you mean?" she protested. "It takes two people to hold each other. You didn't force me to — "

"That's not it!" Todd snapped. His fingers raked his hair. "I'm sorry, Amy. I didn't mean to yell at you." Todd cradled her cheek in his hand. "I love you so much."

Amy gave a little cry. "Then what — ?"

"Sssh," he begged her. His eyes filled with pain. Tenderly, he eased her down onto the rock. He spoke, but his voice sounded like a stranger's. "There's something I have to tell you, too," he said.

Brenda smiled contentedly at Colin over The Left Bank menu. The workshop was over. Everyone was thrilled it had gone so well.

"What kind of omelet was it that Amy liked so much?" Brenda asked. Colin winced, hearing

Amy's name. Brenda wanted to stuff the question back in her mouth.

The boy waiting to take the order looked stiff and hurried.

"Cheese and mushroom," Colin said to Brenda. "Mmmm."

Colin held up two fingers to show the waiter he wanted the same kind. "And two warm croissants with butter," Colin called after him.

Brenda's cheeks were as red as apples when he looked at her again. "I'm sorry," she said. "I didn't mean to bring up any bad stuff."

Colin waved a protest, but he looked uncomfortable. Brenda hesitated. "What time's she coming home?" she asked, spreading her napkin on her lap.

Colin crumpled his. "You mean, *is* she coming home?" His napkin opened slowly in front of him. "You want to know what it was that set me off last night?" he asked suddenly.

"The phone call, I thought — "

"No! That's what's so rotten!" Colin leaned across the table. "I'd just about gotten over that. I kept telling myself I couldn't be sure what was going on, so I'd better just cool it." He sat back. Brenda waited for him to speak. "Then I saw a photograph Dee had taken at the wedding. A shot of Amy" — Colin's mouth twisted — "and some *guy* — dancing *very* closely."

"Did Marc show it to you?" Brenda asked angrily.

"No." Colin's shoulders sagged wearily. He explained what had happened.

Brenda paused to think. "Okay," she admitted.

159

"It doesn't look good." She reached over and grasped Colin's hand. "But life's strange, Mr. Edwards. It flips on you when you least expect it. Maybe something good will come out of all this." The waiter set down their order. She nodded a thank-you at him and checked her watch. "It's two-thirty, right?"

Colin glanced at the clock on the wall. "Right," he said flatly.

"Then, let's see," she said. She stabbed a mushroom with her fork and held it poised in midair. She pretended to concentrate. "According to my calculations, by eight o'clock tonight you could be dancing on Cloud Nine. It's going to be a great homecoming, isn't it?" She chewed the mushroom and swallowed it, and Colin couldn't keep from smiling.

Chapter
19

Amy's face was streaked with pain. "What?" she said. She tried to steady her voice, but she felt as if she'd just been punched in the stomach.

Todd didn't respond. He walked the few steps to the edge of the lake and stood beside it, looking out. To Amy, his back was a solid wall.

She felt frozen, as if she'd never in her life be able to move again, to so much as blink. Even her tears wouldn't spill. Sure, she thought it was funny that Todd hadn't talked that much about his life at college. But a *girl friend*?!

She would not cry. Even though her throat and eyes were burning for her to. Even though she'd been such a dumb, romantic idiot.

"Amy?" Todd said. She stiffened like a board. He was still looking out over the lake. His voice sounded flat and far away. "You know you're not being fair, don't you?"

Now it was her turn not to answer. Todd turned slowly. He came to sit beside her.

"Let me explain again," he said. His eyes pleaded with her to listen.

"You don't owe me an explanation!"

Todd sat up sharply. "I know that!" he snapped. "My not telling you about Nina was no worse than your not telling me about — "

"Colin," Amy finished. It felt strange saying Colin's name now. After all that had happened she didn't feel she had the right.

Todd repeated. His face went soft. "I just want you to understand what I'm feeling, Amy. I want you to believe I didn't mean to hurt you." His voice quivered with emotion. Then it trailed away. "It was just that. . . ."

"What?" Amy said quietly. She felt herself beginning to thaw — enough so she could listen.

"What I feel for you is so different from what I had with Nina." Todd's words rushed out. "I already told you how I felt when I saw you Friday" — Todd's eyes were shining now, remembering — "that we were connected. Not that we *would* connect, but that we were already linked in a thousand ways."

Amy nodded. She'd felt the same.

"Nina, well — " Todd went on haltingly. "I just met her in May. We only had that last month at school to get to know each other." He looked straight at Amy. "So it's not like she's been my girl friend since I was thirteen, or anything." He shrugged. "She's not into the country and animals the way you are. We don't laugh quite as much. But she listens and she cares, and, before I met you, I'd been thinking about her this summer — she's in Italy studying art history. But I wanted to see what would happen this fall when we both got back to school."

"And now?" Amy's voice was small and whispery.

Todd shook his head wistfully. He ran his hand along Amy's back and looked at her. "I feel off-balance — as if I've lost my center."

A faint smile crossed Amy's face. She felt sad, but excited, too, to be talking so openly about her feelings. This was a first for her. If only she'd been able to open up earlier — with Colin. Now she didn't know if she'd ever have that chance.

Suddenly, she felt a knew kind of closeness for Todd. It was strange. They seemed new to each other, as if they'd just been introduced. The image was that they'd come to a fork in the road. Before, they'd taken one road. Now they would take the other.

Amy let her eyes wander. All weekend, the only thing she'd really seen was Todd. The lake and hills and meadow had been no more than a romantic setting. Now they were more. A butterfly rested on a cattail. Its black and orange wings were dazzling. The blue of a dragonfly buzzing around Todd's leg was the color of her scarf. Amy sighed happily. Even though she and Todd were not in each other's arms, the day still shone.

She had no words yet for the feelings swimming around inside her. She was new at talking from the heart.

Realizing that, a wave of sadness swept over her. It didn't seem fair. You learned something.

163

Then life didn't wait for you to use it where you wanted to. There was so much she wanted to tell Todd — and Colin.

"Well," Todd said. He stood and eased her up beside him. "If we don't get that car of mine on the road soon, you may never make it home."

Amy plucked a burr off his white shorts and smiled at him.

They fixed the tire in no time. In the car, on the way home, Todd took Amy's hand after they'd been driving for a while. A warm, strong feeling had replaced the tingles. The calm was easy to take after all the worry and excitement.

"Do you know how I drove myself crazy this weekend?" Amy said.

"You?"

"Me," Amy growled good-naturedly. "I didn't have the slightest idea how I was going to tell you about Colin." She balled her hands into fists. "Why do I get so stupid and worry like that?"

Todd looked over. He grinned. "Cause you're not perfect," he said. " — Like me."

"Oh, is *that* it?" Amy teased. "I wasn't sure."

She stared out the window. The hot summer wind swept her hair around her face. Eventually, she recognized some familiar landmarks: the gas station just outside of town, an ice-cream parlor she'd been to once with Colin, a store where she'd bought a pair of hand-crafted silver earrings.

Rose Hill. Her home. She tired to push the troubling question out of her mind. Would Colin be waiting for her? She'd gone much farther away from him than seventy miles. Suddenly, she couldn't wait to see him.

She lay her head back on the seat and closed her eyes. Todd reached over and touched her hair. She hardly felt his hand.

"Pull in here for a minute, will you?" Amy said five minutes later. Todd had driven onto Rosemont Blvd. It would be another few blocks before he reached the road that would take them to her house.

A Volkswagen was lurching out of a space down the street from The Left Bank Café. Todd glanced questioningly at Amy but he didn't say anything until he slipped into the empty parking space.

"What are we doing here?" he asked lightly. He switched off the ignition.

Amy felt at peace how. It didn't matter that she didn't understand what had happened between them.

She wanted to throw her arms around him — this boy she'd known for so short a time, this person she'd invested so much feeling in. She wanted to tell him what was in her heart.

As usual, Todd understood. He bent close to her. His dark, kind eyes searched her face, and she held tightly to his hand.

Her words came out slowly and quietly. "I want you to know I'm not mad at you — "

Todd threw back his head and laughed. "I sort of figured that," he teased tenderly.

"There's so much more I want to tell you," she went on.

"Hey." Todd touched her arm. "We read each other's minds, remember?"

Color rose in Amy's cheeks. "I'm just going to

miss you," she said, "so much. The awful thing is — " Her mind and heart were off on a wild run suddenly. Her eyes brimmed with tears. She managed to grin through them.

"What?" Todd asked soothingly. He hugged her.

"We're not going to have a chance to test out the 'new us'!" Amy half laughed. The tears started spilling then. "I feel so close to you now. In a way, I feel closer to you than I did when — " Red flamed in her cheeks again.

Todd's eyes were full of feeling. "We could write — " he said huskily.

Amy sat back in her seat. She felt dizzy. Oh, how she wanted to tell Todd yes — yes, they could write, they could write every day if they wanted to.

But this new feeling they'd found was just that — *new,* too new to be trusted to put out all the old fires. "We can't," she told him. Her voice was so faint, it seemed that someone far away from her had said the words.

Todd smiled sadly. Amy knew he understood what would happen if they wrote. They'd be killing the chances of really living their own lives. One foot would always be out the door. For a long time, just seeing Todd's name on a return address would bring back too many fiery memories.

Todd was playing with her garnet pinky ring. She reached out to touch his cheek. Suddenly she gasped. All the feeling drained out of her. Brenda and Colin were walking arm in arm toward the town parking lot from The Left Bank. Amy shivered.

166

"Home?" Todd said gently. His expression told her something was wrong. He squeezed her hand.

"Yes," she murmured. Her heart ached. She was relieved when Todd started the engine. When they drove away, she could breathe again.

She turned around in her seat as they passed the lot, her eyes fixed on Colin. She shuddered, seeing Brenda kiss him on the cheek. The next moment, Todd's hand was on her back to steady her.

"Don't look so worried," he said.

She flickered a reassuring smile, but she felt as if her heart had been wrung dry.

Even before, with Brenda's lips on his cheek, Colin felt as if he were standing alone. He'd seen Amy and the guy from the wedding photograph sitting in the car. Out of the corner of his eye, he'd watched them drive past.

Now he sat in the Bronco. He felt sick, suddenly, and weary. In frustration, he banged the steering wheel with the bottom of his fist. The horn blasted.

He leaned on the wheel, pressed his head to his arm. Slowly, it dawned on him he might never hold Amy in his arms again. The odds were a million to one she wanted to be with another guy. But he wouldn't let that happen! Sitting up abruptly, he flicked on the ignition, and the engine kicked over. How could he stand it? This was *Amy* he was losing. *Amy*. Panic raced through him. He drove out of the parking lot, tires squealing. *Amy*. He loved her so much, he knew his heart would never let her go. Somehow he'd find a way for them to be together again. He'd risk everything. He'd talk to her — really *talk* and see what could happen when he opened up. The worst would be that it wouldn't make a difference. But the best — the *best*? Colin smiled slightly. Then he shivered. The hope he felt suddenly both comforted and frightened him.

Chapter
20

Dee pedaled as fast as she could toward Rosemont Park, perspiration collecting on the collar of her sleeveless T-shirt. Amy had sounded reasonably calm on the phone — but desperate, too, as if the two feelings were battling inside her.

Now, seeing her friend waiting by the covered bridge, Dee had no idea what would happen.

Amy pulled her off her bike and hugged her.

"Let me guess," Dee said, eyeing her. "You're going crazy."

Amy grinned, and nodded vigorously. "I had to get out of the house," She said between gritted teeth. "Every time the phone rang — every time the doorbell sounded, I thought it might be Colin." She flopped down by the bank of the stream. "I think my heart stopped at least ten times today. Dee," she said, gazing at her friend, "thanks for meeting me. I don't know what I would have done if you didn't come."

Dee's mind was spinning. On the way to the park, she'd promised herself she wouldn't take sides. Colin was a good friend, too. But now Amy was obviously counting on her. "Whoa," Dee said kindly. "Don't forget, I'm Colin's friend, too."

"I know," Amy said.

"So — " Dee prompted, "Let's talk."

"This could take a while," Amy warned.

Dee shrugged. "I've got a long life ahead of me. I think I can share a piece of it with you." She glued her eyes to Amy's face and gave her a faint smile.

Amy started explaining. She told Dee about the entire weekend, including how it ended. When she was done, she placed her hand over her chest. "Oh, Dee." Her voice cracked when she spoke. "I feel like my heart is really breaking. I know I don't deserve to have Colin back, but I miss him." Slowly, she lowered her head and looked at Dee.

Dee's eyes narrowed. "And it's not just because Todd isn't around?"

Amy didn't answer right away. She'd asked herself that question over and over all day long. "No," she said deliberately. "Because I love him."

"Keep going."

Amy skimmed her hand over the stiff, dry grass. "Because he's — he was — real."

Dee looked puzzled. "Wasn't Todd real?"

"No. I mean, yes. Oh, Dee, I'm not sure *what* I mean!"

Dee's heart swelled with compassion. Amy seemed so genuinely confused.

"I can't sort it all out!" Amy blurted. "On Friday, I loved Colin. On Saturday, I loved Todd. Actually, I think I loved them both. What do you think about that?!" Her eyes glistened with pain.

"Oh, Amy, I don't know! I don't see how you can really love two guys at the same time. But with love, maybe anything's possible." Dee hesitated. "I just hope — "

"Hope what?"

"That you don't want Colin back now just because you're frightened."

Amy's voice was low. She shook her head. "That would be awful. But I don't think that's what's happening."

Dee was silent. She propped herself against a tree stump and twiddled with a piece of grass she'd plucked. She couldn't help it — her thoughts were straying to Colin now. Suddenly, she wondered if Marc had broken his promise and interfered.

Amy sighed deeply.

Dee looked at her. "What *is* happening?" she said.

Amy took another deep breath. She leaned back on her elbows. "In Elk Spring," she began, "I felt as if I were in another world. A fairyland. I met Todd, and he — " Amy felt choked with memories. " — He was so perfect, Dee. I could talk to him the way I never had been able to talk with Colin."

"Why?" Dee sat up and crossed her legs under her.

"I think, because I knew I'd probably never see him again. He was my prince. He was safe. If I

171

made a fool of myself, it wouldn't matter. It wouldn't affect my relationship because — " she spoke in a quiet voice, "because we didn't *have* a real relationship."

"What *did* you have?"

Amy's eyes got misty. "I don't know — I guess we had a dream."

"Do you think you could talk with Colin now, the way you did with Todd?"

"I'm not sure." A silly expression spread over Amy's face. "Todd and I said good-bye before I had time enough to practice."

Dee laughed.

"Anyway, if Colin and I start changing the way we talk to each other, something tells me I'd have to be the teacher." Amy gulped away a rush of tears. "But it doesn't matter. I don't think I'll have the chance to try."

Dee scowled. "What are you talking about?"

Amy's eyes filled up again. "I think that the same thing that happened to me in Elk Spring may have happened to Colin right here in Rose Hill. She wiped her eyes. "I think that while I was gone he fell for Brenda Austin."

"Are you crazy?" Dee gripped Amy's shoulders.

"I've had a bad feeling all along . . . and I saw them, Dee."

"What are you talking about? You saw them? Where?"

"In town, while Todd was driving me home. Brenda was holding onto his arm on their way to the parking lot. They'd just come out of The Left Bank Café — that's *our* place, Dee!"

"*Your* place?" Dee exclaimed. "Nobody else is allowed to go there?"

Amy's expression darkened. "Don't be dumb. You know what I mean." She paused. " — and Brenda kissed him."

"Where did she kiss him?"

"In the parking lot."

"That's *not* what I mean, Amy. Did she kiss him on the mouth?"

"No — "

Dee rolled her eyes. "Then why are you so sure something's really wrong?"

Amy looked away. She didn't want to answer Dee's question. She didn't want to analyze her feelings anymore. All she wanted now was to be in Colin's arms — to see how that felt. She couldn't swear she'd feel the same way about him. But how could she know without seeing him again? She felt Dee's hand on hers.

"Give him time," Dee said. "Look. . . ." She cringed, seeing the pain on her friend's face. "You may not agree with this, but I think everything will work out."

Amy managed a smile. "Since when did you turn psychic?"

Dee's eyes danced with mischief. "You think *you're* the only one who can learn something new?" She stood up and brushed dirt off the back of her legs. "Really, Amy." She looked down at her friend. "You and Colin had something good. Everybody knew that."

"They did?" Amy clung to that thought like a life raft.

Dee stretched a smile from ear to ear. "Yeah. So quit worrying. You have very smart friends." She rapped Amy's head with her knuckles and tossed her a stick of gum from out of her pocket.

"Now go on home," Dee told her. "Dig in your garden or something. It's seven o'clock. There's still some light left."

Colin sat numbly in front of his computer. He'd been trying to get a head start on the workshop evaluation that he and Marc and Dick Westergard would be doing. The computer monitor flickered, but all Colin saw on the screen was Amy's face.

What if everything his eyes had told him earlier had been a lie? Maybe he and Amy could still be good together. Colin shook his head in frustration. He exited the computer and flicked it off. Right now, he didn't see how that would be possible.

Stretching, he leaned back in his chair, cupping his hands behind his head. He thought back to Friday night, at Brenda's. There had been a moment when he had wanted to hold her, to kiss her.

She'd stopped him cold. They'd talked about the feeling, and the feeling died.

Colin rubbed his temples. In that instant with Brenda, he hadn't stopped loving Amy — he simply wasn't thinking of her. And now he understood something. How a person — a good person like Amy — could end up for a while in someone else's arms.

"Hey, Amy!" Susan called from the back porch. "You going to sleep out there?"

"No," Amy said.

The back door closed quietly, and she returned to her digging. It was dusk. Sam was right beside her. Susan and her mother were in the house, but she felt very alone.

She kept working the soil, even though she could hardly see what she was doing. Every once in a while, she glanced over her shoulder and talked to Sam. "Just one more day, Sammy, puppy. Then the vet will take the bandage off."

She thought of Todd then, about what a fine vet he'd make. She missed him terribly already. The sight of him clunking out of the driveway in his beat-up Chevy had glued her to the step, even after he had gone. She had felt so empty watching him go, as if he'd taken her with him and only her shell was left behind.

Was that the reason she wanted to see Colin? So he could fill the gap that Todd had left? Dee had asked her that. Now her heart told her no.

She squinted to capture the last light, but clouds shifted across the moon and stayed there. Stretching slowly to her feet, she remembered the trowel and bent to look for it. She wiped it with a rag until it shone, then carried it to the tool shed.

Sam started barking furiously just as she locked the shed door. Just as suddenly, he went quiet.

Amy padded toward the backyard as silently as she could. By the light of the street lamp, she saw Colin stooping over Sam, petting him. Her pulse raced. She could hardly catch her breath.

From deep inside her came a huge sigh of relief and longing. Colin heard her and glanced up, his attention fixed on her. At first, she couldn't look at him. Even in the dark, she was afraid of what she might see. Standing near Colin, she felt she'd gone around the world a million times and had only now come home.

The clouds swept past the moon and Amy could see the light reflected in Colin's eyes. She stood motionless, half hidden in the shadows. Her hands hung at her sides, but her arms and back were stiff. Colin would have to make the first move — *she* couldn't.

But then from nowhere, she said, "If you want to break up with me, Colin, I'll understand. *Really.*" She felt like a rock. Her tears were buried deep.

Colin put his fingers to his lips. Amy's cheeks flushed when he rose to his feet and approached her. He quickened his pace for the last few steps. Amy flung open her arms and he rushed into them.

His scent, his touch, all her memories of him came flooding back. Amy gasped when he lifted her feet off the ground. When he swung her, she clung to him fiercely.

There was so much to say, Amy realized, yet so much that could never be fully explained. She would try to make her feelings clear. She promised herself that. But now, she pulled back. Her eyes devoured every inch of Colin's face. His expression said enough for now, convincing her that talk could wait.

Later in her room, she unpacked the small suitcase she'd taken to Andrea's. Sam hobbled in. She took a minute to pet him. Then she ran her fingers across the blue scarf Colin had given her. It was draped over her chair. Amy smiled wistfully. Now it seemed less like a scarf and more like a promise.

Nothing could guarantee love's lasting — she knew that. Todd was gone now. She might not have Colin forever. But then again, and Amy's heart filled as she gazed at the glowing moon outside her window, maybe, just maybe, she would.

Coming Soon
Couples #25
LOVE EXCHANGE

Amy looked for Colin in the kitchen, where Greg reported having seen him last, but all she found was another tray of tacos and a large bowl of ice. Then she tried the basement, where she found Karen Davis and Rich Edwards sorting through his father's record collection. From there she tried the living room, but it was clear that the action had moved onto the patio. Only a few party stragglers, either talking or eating, remained inside.

Sliding open the glass doors to the patio, Amy was just in time to see Colin dance by with Kirsten in his arms. He looked positively enthralled. Amy's heart skipped a beat.

Quietly, she slipped back into the house. She didn't want Colin to see her watching him. Sinking on to the couch, Amy told herself she'd just have to wait it out. Reaching into a bowl next to the couch, Amy began to munch on a handful of chips.

Brian had slipped back even further into the past; he was now playing an Elvis Presley song that was sweet, slow, and romantic. Getting to her feet, she headed for the patio again. All at once she knew she'd been silly to doubt Colin's affection for her. He was just being a good host to the Swedish exchange students; that was all. Lighten up, she told herself.

She searched the faces for Colin, wanting more than anything to dance with him. Pushing her way through the crowd, she spotted the back of his blond hair. It was definitely him. Eagerly, she moved closer. She was about to tap him on the shoulder when she saw he already had a girl in his arms. Not just any girl, though. Now he was dancing with Ilse Munsson.

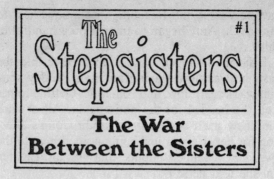

#1

The Stepsisters

The War
Between the Sisters

by Tina Oaks

Chapter Excerpt

Paige Whitman unzipped the plastic cover that held the dress she was to wear to her father's wedding. She had put off looking at the dress until the very last minute. When she learned the dress would be pink, she had groaned. There were colors she loved, colors she could take or leave alone, and then there was pink, which hated her as much as she hated it!

And the style was as impossible for her as the color. She didn't even have to try the dress on to know how it would look. At sixteen she was taller than most of her friends, and thinner without being really skinny. But taller meant longer, and she knew her neck was too long to wear a low, rounded neckline like that.